OUR NAPOLEON IN RAGS

A NOVEL

Kirby Gann

Brooklyn, NY

OUR NAPOLEON IN RAGS

© 2005 Kirkby Gann Tittle

Ig Publishing
178 Clinton Ave.
Brooklyn, NY 11205

www.igpub.com

LIBRARY OF CONGRESS CATALOGING-IN-PUBLICATION DATA

Gann, Kirby, 1968–
    Our Napoleon in rags : a novel / by Kirby Gann.— 1st ed.
        p. cm.
    ISBN 0-9752517-3-2 (alk. paper)
    1. Politicians—Family relationships—Fiction. 2. Bars (Drinking
establishments)—Fiction. 3. Manic-depressive persons—Fiction.
4. Male prostitutes—Fiction. 5. Middle West—Fiction. 6. Gay youth—
Fiction. I. Title.
    PS3607.A55O94 2005
    813'.6—dc22

                                        2005001686

10-digit ISBN: 0-9752517-3-2
13-digit ISBN: 978-0-9752517-3-2

Cover image by P. Dean Pearson
Cover and text design by Kirby Gann

Printed in Canada
This book is printed on acid-free paper.

10 9 8 7 6 5 4 3 2 1
FIRST EDITION

For Stephanie

CONTENTS

TRAILING
WINDMILL
SAILS

THE NIGHTS AT THE DON QUIXOTE
– that sumptuous dive – held darker than nights elsewhere, even if the club sat huddled within the smacked heart of the city. As in the rest of America (and for most Americans), this heart rarely became an object of attention and care, more fretted over than attended to, arteries hardening without complaint, a condition forming without the host's knowledge. Like the biological heart, one remained aware but avoided the subject. One leaves the heart alone and hopes for the best.

We are in Old Towne, the broken-streetlight district in Montreux where dark house-stoops offer no welcome. Most of the light that sparked through the leaded wave windows of the Don Q was of the flashing variety, red and blue and sometimes white – vascular colors. The regulars called the Don Q the heart of Old Towne, thus making it the heart within the heart.

The original, stately farmhouse had once sat well outside city limits in 1865. As the decades passed it suffered add-ons and reconstruction to the point of invisibility, subsumed by brick. In our own time, the Don Quixote fell victim to the *Come Back to Montreux!* campaign, that brief resuscitation effort sponsored by the city council in the 1980s. They slashed mortgage rates in the vain effort to stave urban sprawl, inviting the wealthy to reinvest in squalid mansions left over from a more elegant era. Everyone believed Old Towne should have been the crown jewel to the city, a Dresden captured in amber glass on the muddy Ohio bank to lure tourists up from the Charleston and Savannah wastelands. But that support was arrested by a number of awful events, acts between the poor and dissolute confronted by the moneyed's sudden interest, a history better left to sociologists studying the consequences of strikes, assaults, rapes, and murder. The campaign restored a few strewn blocks of eclectic architecture, but most of the homes remained arsoned-empty, or skinned by molding scaffolding, the hides of plastic sheets. What was left were hookers of all specialties and interests; adult bookstores barking private video booths; men in raincoats skipping over splashed glass in the streets, headed for the pawnshop brokers and liquor stores protected by pig-iron bars. And the Don Quixote, ferned and atriumed toward the glittering stars.

A wicket gate and garden path led to the entrance, crowned by a ragged windmill that was useless but for effect. Inside, the tiled floor swept down five quick stairs onto a mahogany and teak sunken bar. Above, in the original farmhouse, stretched the Theatre Room, where unsung playwrights presented works-in-progress, poets of the rant school sieged the stage for endless hours, and bands of every style played deep into the night. Though somewhat devout Christians, Beau and Glenda Stiles (the owners) still harbored bits of Bohemian soul.

Near the sunken bar there, under corroded lattice-work and paper lamps put up for sale by a Third World economic savior organization, Haycraft Keebler parlayed his days. As did Glenda and Beau, with their hapless helpmeet Mather Williams; as did the half-Cuban Romeo Díaz and his love Anantha Bliss, and even "our cop" Chesley Sutherland – all of whom own their places in this story, too.

Beau and Glenda provided the body the rest moved within, but Haycraft Keebler was the heart in the heart in the heart of this city. Or, to keep with the metaphor of the place, draw the group as a windmill with Hay the hub, the rest reaching sails – because Haycraft *was* the history of the place; his family blood was. His ancestors had settled the land and built the house, saw it lose the farm-field vistas as the old drive was first scarfed by dirt road, then cobblestones, then pavement, up to the day in Haycraft's adolescence when corruption charges were leveled against his legendary father. The family sold the house and fled to Tennessee.

The celebrated mayor of Montreux in wartime, renowned for his string ties and classical learning, his passion for the arts and the planting of dogwoods; the holder of a congressional seat, who had been awarded a bronze statue in Frederick Park for his dedication to the progress of his community – Haycraft's father Edmund Keebler expired before his family in a splash of his own vomit. Perhaps for this reason Haycraft became the crusader he was, seriously disturbed if unaccountably charming. *Our bipolar bear*, the regulars called him.

Whether keeping with his lithium or not, whether coherent in his rhetorical oratorios or else slurred manic to the point of raving, Haycraft believed in the agency of a long-gone Old Towne community, believed it with feverish religiosity, refusing to acknowledge that community's extinction, recognizing however its dormancy. This conviction had forced him through a life of perpetual crises and La Manchian quests, of plangent hours sired by doubt and solitude. Yet throughout all difficulties Hay knew he could transform the world.

And on this night, the night when this story starts, he shouldered his satchel beneath the windmill and through the double doors with ardent certainty that the first baby steps toward that transformation were now taken, enacted in the sabotage of a public bus.

Haycraft had his own philosophy, his own methods.

—You are over twenty minutes late. I was beginning to worry, we were going to send Chesley out to look for you, cried Glenda at the sight of him.

Haycraft hurried to her with gracious smile and nodding head, waddling down the steps to the sunken bar with an ache in his back.

— No need at all, no need for worries, Glenda, I am perfectly fine. An evening of action. Resolving the question of character and fortitude and all of that.

He beamed into the face of the older woman, a face like a peach too ripe, swollen fat yet sunken in patches; a once-sweet face gone sour.

— You should tell me of all people if you've adjusted your schedule, Hay. I do have my own anxieties –

— Yes, Glenda, it was thoughtless of me. Just a touch behind. And of course you have your anxieties; here, let me give you a little something for your troubles.

Haycraft opened the withered flap of his oilcloth satchel and scrounged through one of the interior pockets. He cast a glance back up the stairs at Chesley Sutherland, who was a cop, a true working cop, although at the moment he was on leave pending an investigation of his behavior and was thus moonlighting as security for Beau and Glenda. Sutherland made a show of fiddling with the dials of his police scanner (an off-duty hobby, a way of keeping up with the trade), and Haycraft stole two blue pills from the satchel and handed them over the bar.

— You are a dear boy, Glenda said; she caressed his hand once and disappeared behind the swinging saloon doors that led to the kitchen behind the bar.

The row of regulars watched her leave. None of them offered

comment. Her husband wiped down the teak of the counter with a damp hand towel as he set out a pint of English ale for Haycraft – his eyes, pouched in beer-gut pads, following Glenda until she was out of earshot.

— What will those do to her?

— A couple of smiles, nothing more, answered Haycraft. She will be calm tonight, my friend. No nagging for you; no agitation.

Haycraft knew agitation like an old friend; he knew anxiety the way the stable mind knows when it's time to flee a scene. Rigorous schedules helped him *maintain*: the wristwatch looped through his belt gave specific measure to where he was in his timetable, pointing him also to where he should be without the allowance of delays. And Beau and Glenda knew that schedule well: three hours of meditative writing, three hours to canvass the Old Towne district registering voters (or taking action against the community's latest outrage-in-common), thirty-five minutes for the tending of needs such as grocery shopping and basic grooming. Afterward he liked to pass one hour and fifteen minutes with the homeless men who played chess on the iron-slat benches near the library, offering them bananas and squash, an assortment of nuts – Haycraft steered clear of the passionately colored foods, preferring the calm safety of earth tones. Each evening he proceeded in haste to the Don Quixote for his beer, his studies, and chance companionship.

He did not worry for work. Being dramatically bipolar and publicly registered as such, the government sent checks that he signed over to Beau Stiles, who acted as something of a guardian. The agreement being that Beau would hand over the money in increments (Haycraft could not fathom the responsibility of a bank account), ensuring that the fundamental expenses were covered first: rent, utilities, pharmaceuticals, et cetera. But Beau was a busy if good-hearted man, and more often than not he cashed the check at his own register and forked over one lump sum of bar-damp bills with the order *Now Hay, don't you go manic with all this in your pocket.* Haycraft swore to a regimen of acute self-diligence; but – also more often than not – he would skip doses of medication (testing how long he could go without, when feeling well) and hit a spell before the cash found the land-lord, or the gas and electric company, and a tip jar would appear at the corner of the bar with a strip of masking tape across the glass, Hay's Rent inscribed in permanent marker. Beau covered the rest when he could. Beau said he never had cared to live as a rich man.

Haycraft remained aware of the debt he owed such charity.

— Beau Stiles, if and when I begin to play the lottery, and if I were ever to find myself reveling in the good fortune of such unlikely victory, you may rest assured you will receive my entire first year of deposit. I swear on that!

— We need two hundred K to get clear. Be sure to pick your numbers before the next full moon, we could both use health insurance.

Such loyalty originated in shared family history. As a young man Beau played bluegrass with Haycraft's father – Beau on bass, Representative Keebler on fiddle – and he and Glenda had been there as bystanders when the connection to the race track was discovered, investigated, publicized, et cetera; they had watched sadly as the bright child Haycraft used to be developed into the strange soul the regulars knew. Beau felt some measure of responsibility for the tragedy, too, as he had led the retinue that brought Hay's father to the horses.

He tried to look out for Edmund's son, though it was not always easy. He had this place, a haven for the man, he would like to say; if he could, he would like to tell his old friend that his son was doing all right, that he was doing as best he could.

But the Don Q was not always the great refuge Beau hoped to create or Haycraft hoped to find. Hulking Chesley Sutherland eased down the stairs cradling his radio close to his cheek, the volume swept low to a bare crackle and burst.

— Yo Haycraft, you hear what I'm talking about? Bus crash tonight, four blocks down on Second. Guy pushes junk out in the street and wrecks a bus. Took out three parked cars and some lady.

— I can assure you I don't know the first thing about it, Chesley. You said a lady? What do you mean, is she all right?

— They didn't make a formal announcement. They got an ambulance there is what I know. What've you been up to? I notice you come up late.

— Leave him alone, said Romeo Díaz. Let the guy be, Sutherland, you're not even on the force these days.

— Not today, no, but I will be again, you know. And I'll have my eye on you, too, Díaz.

— Buses crash, officer, answered Romeo. It's a tough world out there.

— Garbage doesn't just fall into the street. Somebody put it there, they shoved it there. I think I know somebody.

— You don't know anybody, man, you need me to tell you that?

Haycraft made a point of examining the yellow suds clinging to the insides of his pint glass.

— Yes, Haycraft said. Buses do crash all the time, don't they? It *is* a dangerous neighborhood, you know. I think it a shame you are not allowed at the moment to keep us safe, Chesley; perhaps I'll explore that in an upcoming editorial. All kinds of crazies running around.

The notion of becoming the subject of Keebler's obscure essays did not impress Sutherland in the least.

— Yeah, your editorial. You put that in there, I'll take it to my hearing.

— It could help! Discernible proof that the community stands behind you!

But this was said more as an aside, an afterthought. Haycraft's head was already on to other things: After the day's modest action, and the growing certainty that he may have gotten away with it, he could be forgiven the rush building inside him, his emotions insurgent and mutinous, the roilsome confidence that identified him (he felt certain) as a brash leader of men. This notion of "a lady" hurt – maybe even killed? – because of his actions was quickly morphing from an object of guilty fright to one of fateful purpose:

— I do hope your old woman is all right, of course. But maybe her misfortune is precisely what we need to inspire people to action. This district, what we need is a catalyst, Hay postulated. Something to fuse our determination, firm our resolve. A symbol, an icon, an issue to gather the many into one. *A martyr....* Old Towne is a dangerous community, a community *in danger*; we need nothing less than a crusade. Crusades produce martyrs.

— We've had enough of martyrs here, Beau reminded Hay, curling a dry tongue over white-whiskered lips.

— Yes, but maybe this *lady....* Haycraft trailed off.

He had no comeback; he knew Beau had it pegged: The two boys from St. Luke's High School had created no catalyst to a saving crusade six years before. Instead they had started the engine behind Old Towne's hastened decline. Lost one night on their way to a football game, they ended up in a discarded alleyway freezer – a block behind the Don Q in Huddle Gate Square – with trousers about their ankles, hands bound, one bullet wound each at the base of the skull. It had been Beau Stiles who found them. White suburban kids raped and murdered, killing too any further interest from investors. That the murderers were found at the investigation's fever pitch, and were both black, unemployed, had previous violent records and contraband pasts the legal system had let slip through – locals, in other words – did nothing to encourage the moneyed public to find more to salvage there. Charming, once-lavish houses, yes; but little else. An area beyond salvation.

In his dark moments even Haycraft admitted that, for the most part, they were right. Still he said: *All the more reason. All the more reason to try again. And yet again, if need be.*

— Victory to the persevering, Romeo Díaz gave as a mocking toast. Haycraft, we need to get your candle dipped, man. We need to get you laid.

— You guys have all the plans, added Beau, casting the line out to everyone in a row at the bar, setting hacking cackles among the rank of men.

Romeo Díaz still held that sex was liberation; Haycraft knew the act would never erase the effect of Beau's discovery that long-ago morning. That one of the murderers was also first cousin to Mather Williams provided endless fascination to Haycraft. By nature, fascination came easily to him: His soft lips fell into their curious fold, as of a horse's mouth, loose, parted in rapt concentration, his eyes open and unblinking at whatever matter required his attention.

Glenda Stiles had made herself a kind of patron to Mather, a gentle but damaged soul, *touched* (people said), a man of general incapabilities. She called him a Child of God. Haycraft watched thin black Mather shuffle-muttering about the Don Quixote's rooms in a swaybacked, knock-kneed gait, singing to himself, his mop standing in for a microphone. Hay observed Mather helping Glenda with prep work in the kitchen, the soft dark face lengthened in concentrated scowl, fleshy cheeks loose and shifting, his white server's jacket – a leftover from one of Beau's previous jobs – and black pants splattered with sauces, dips, cleaning agents. Haycraft would watch and ruminate aloud, wondering at what Mather knew about that murderous cousin, about what memories did the two share in common, and how did these affect him now – or did they affect him at all? Did the guy understand *anything?* He knew right from wrong; Mather was all about blessings. What does one make of having a murderer in the family? And when Mather finished his jobs and sat with his shift drink (brandy) on a corner stool at the bar, Haycraft ventured to ask.

— Mather, please, he began. Your cousin....

Except dear damaged Mather declined to talk about it. Maybe he couldn't talk about it. Moments such as these caused Haycraft to lament that anything he wanted to understand succeeded in escaping him. Here is Mather listening: he leans his cauliflowered ear to Hay and his globular eyes spring wide; he tilts backward and shakes his head, says, *No no no, uh-uh,* or dismisses the conversation entirely: *That boy bad from the day he born, we got the devil everywhere you know.* He cackles a discomfiting, high-pitched crow's laugh, rolling those gelato eyes, a sight people found disturbing before they realized his harmlessness. Mather's eyes bulged large, the lids folded back to expose the entire egglike eyeball, glistening white and greasy wet. His teeth were yellowed and gnarled as though he had grown up gnawing bicycle chains. The mouth spread strung with spittle, the pink tongue withdrew as he laughed and laughed.

Haycraft could not find the answer directly, so he took the more roundabout method of examining Mather's posterboard paintings, which dotted the walls throughout the building. Haycraft could spend as much as an hour in front of a single picture, savoring its forms and colors, reading the scrawled texts, absorbing the most minute of details. Primitive, yes; wildly oilstick colorful; splatched in scrawl – the works depicted a psyche lost to the cityscape. Crudely drawn corporate-logo galaxies (Marathon Oil, McDonald's arches, Shell) spun in orbit about cartoon street signs, roadway markers, cars and buses, the occasional train. Scenes from the city set off-kilter, floating on the paper with no concern for perspective. Brooking these images ran rivers of prose, estuaries of free-associative diatribes and rivulet declarations, seemingly transcribed unedited from Mather's head:

THIS is tHe MarATHon, you GoT to run run run to
tHe MarATHon serMon of MatHer WilliaMs
EvrYtHiNG MusT GO! sale. How abOUT tHaT
MoNeY, brotHErs and SISterS? TeLL ME hoW BoUT
SOME HELP? I taKe eAcH BOTtoM DoLLaR.

Mather scratched out the sentences in ballpoint pen or drug-store magic marker, lines aslant at whatever angle struck him as most convenient at the time of composition. And there among intersection road lights and vaguely figurative passersby, Mather designed advertisements for himself: *SonGs For SALE / OnE DoLLAr I SING my oWN SonGs!!!*

A list of titles with recommendations:

1) BathTub Blues – GOOD for winter sorrow
2) ruiNATION day – no child under 6
i mean 7 allowed, this SonG is SCARY
3)Them Dead Rat Blues
4)Somewhere Out on LonGStand RoAD

The last about when he got lost on the bus lines and ended up stranded in the county's far east end. Haycraft paid a dollar to hear him sing that one, once.

Don Q regulars often stumbled across Mather at work, sitting on a street corner singing, surrounded by his art supplies as a child in a romper room, oblivious to the pedestrians and working girls altering paths to put more space around him. When not puttering about as help for Glenda, all Mather did was take the bus to city parts known and unknown. Whatever image caught his eye, whatever thought crossed his mind, made its way into his medium.

Haycraft inspected the works for a sign, a symbol, a clue he could use toward understanding. Chesley Sutherland confessed he could find nothing in them but the distortions of a raving mind. Romeo Díaz could expound on their value as relics of folk art – but the most real thing about Romeo was that he believed all art a sham, a con his nature allowed him in on the game of. Beau admired their energy, thought they proved the man had soul. And Haycraft agreed, arguing that even if the works could not be regarded as Fine Art headed for future museums, they still displayed a specific vitality. He pegged Mather as a kind of warped antenna, channeling the energy from the streets and setting down messages from the collective, communal spirit of place.

— Because you can see nothing contrived in them, he said. Nothing fabricated. They feel urgent and necessary, and what better definition of art can you devise on your own?

Once Mather finished his single brandy he said his farewells: a process that took a great deal of time. He repeated his farewells with a string of *Thank you Glenda*'s, and *Were you happy with me today*'s, and *Do you want me back tomorrow*'s, all to which Glenda gently responded with *Yes, Mather, thank you too, we'll see you here tomorrow*. It was ritual, perfected over years. He took her hand into both of his, delivered a smile and some speech; and then it was Mather walking two steps before turning again with the *Were you happy with me today?*, a hesitation as he listened to her assurances, and then again a few more steps away before he returned to see if he should come back tomorrow, back and forth, again and again. Only after he passed the luckless bar line of regulars did he say goodbye to each. He navigated the six steps from the sunken bar using an unpleasant seesaw movement with his hips, a walk that looked like he carried a great weight, as if he struggled to carry some object larger than himself. At the top he met Chesley Sutherland, who leaned into the exposed-brick wall with arms crossed over a once-banded, now meaty chest.

— And how are you today, my brother? A good day?

Chesley answered only with a smirk and tip of his head.

— You keep breathing right, now, Mather added, gesturing at

the asthma inhaler Sutherland clutched in one hand. You got to be strong, you got to be strong to be blessed, you know what I'm saying? Be blessed with a breathe-right night now.

Mather raised one hand in gentle beneficence as a gesture of goodbye-good will. Then, his eyes and jaw swooping over a long arc back to the others:

— You *all* have yourselves a blessed night now.

And off he went into the city evening, alone, to wherever it was he lived or hid, or to take his seat on one of the Montreux buses going anywhere.

With Mather gone and the click of the door stays fitting one another behind him, a settling descended over the rooms as the regulars relaxed into their long-haul night.

Capture this: Hoagy Carmichael whispers through the overhead speakers of the main parlor (one rests near Beau's cracked stand-up bass, a holdover from his bluegrass days), its light piano lilting through "I Get Along Without You Very Well" as Romeo's no-filters sift blue smoke about the pentagram paper lanterns; Romeo shifts in a single-breasted sport jacket, his benjamin overcoat thrown lightly over the bar and his Stacies propped on the stool next to him, all animated gesture and argument to Beau, who stands in rolled shirtsleeves pretending to listen. A clement smile graces Beau's lips, he clutches a wash rag in one hand, and he directs his eyes to the baseball game on TV. Glenda murmurs the melody while she folds cloth napkins in contented lassitude, her floral smock reeking dusted with spices and sauce, her bobbed hair caught on one side in the arm of her eyeglasses; Chesley Sutherland sidles down the steps, rubbing the ginger stubble on his head and resituating the holster over his hip as he cranes around a post to catch the score. A few couples splay scattered and intent over their tables. Upstairs in the Theatre Room, the night's band begins to check their levels, the drummer giving a shy punch to his kick.

Haycraft watches them. His lips part slightly, eyes saucer huge behind thick lenses, two fingers the size and texture of sausages holding his place in a fat book. He stares at the room and then the window, falling deep into the light outside as it grows fine as sand, whirling with red and blue, singing with descending sirens; soon that light filters to black, and the reflection of the bar in the glass stretches narrowly into the leaf-dusted, bottle-strewn boulevard. The illusion of the bar extending into the streets is definitive to Haycraft: All his efforts were focused on bringing the strangely patient camaraderie from inside the building out to spread over the neighborhood, and to bring the people from outside, in.

Capture this picture in a long slow dissolve, these few souls held static in their particular share of solitude. They offer singular visions of companionship to whomever happens along. A picture hesitant through the following hours, expectant, waiting for midnight to arrive like some longed-for music, waiting for each night to be stirred alive.

§

As the moon reaches its full height, the typical weirdness sets in:

No one could guess why a retired ballerina decided to discard her top and shimmy onto the half-wall that cleaved the bar from the rest of the room. Two AM and her shift finished at the Primrose Girls on the Go-Go, the Don Q parlor nearly crowded with sweating bikers and slumming bankers and career students ravished by their need to break from all things MOM – they shouted again and again for the bourbon and the beer that polished each leering face to a hazy shine.

Beau scurries to serve in Hawaiian shirt and black leather apron. He shouts to Romeo Díaz, *No, no, tell her not here, this is a good place!* and allows himself a good take on her bare torso before casting a glance for any glimpse of wife Glenda nearby; at no sign of her, he hacks a grateful guffaw.

Romeo turns to the young woman to pass on Beau's orders, but stops speechless at the marvel of her bare breasts, sculpted scoops of pale flesh peaked by a maraschino cherry rose. She drifts through a drunken routine of pliés and jètés, culminating with a turned ankle, a surprised exclamation, her bruised bottom scattering dirty glasses from a nearby tray.

She sits in silent rumination, gazes at the floor with a confounded smile. As if alone in her bedroom she reaches to her left breast and scratches the underside softly.

— Buy her whatever she's drinking, a shirtless man in leather jacket, HELLZAPOPPIN emblazoned across the shoulders, waves to Beau. He mocks applause for the performance, shouts his thanks.

— Well what the fuck is that? asks his companion, twenty-three clutching at forty with handbag-leather cheeks and blue smudges beneath her eyes. Smoke frets from her mouth and over his face though she appears to be griping to an invisible associate beside her, loud enough for HELLZAPOPPIN to hear. He fiddles with one of the tiny rubber bands spindling the braids in his beard.

— Let it hang, woman, he answers her.

She sucks harder on her cigarette and hot-boxes it, the yellow of her eyes rimmed with venom. He looks at her, looks away, smacks his lips at something distasteful, looks at her again:

— Don't break my balls over it, jesus, I'll slap you here to Nashville, he adds, and this breaks her gaze.

Díaz approaches the dancer, fresh gin rickey on HELLZAPOPPIN's tab in hand for her. He drapes his jacket over her small, bare shoulders; her top seems to have disappeared. Beau checks Chesley Sutherland, who scowls and shakes his head, setting Beau to wonder if he should expect a crackdown soon – he worries that Chesley, under investigation with another cop for his second excessive-force complaint, might decide tipping off a fruitful bust could help his case with the department. Then again, Chesley still wears his gun, which *can't* be legal in his situation. On such unadmitted bargaining chips Chesley and Beau have built a solid working relationship.

A pack of redneck southenders stride down the six steps from the Theatre Room, exulting in the nostalgia of classic-rock covers going on in there. Swine-eyed with liquor and scavenging for more, a brush-cut boy in Hilfiger attire continues to a buddy:

— I says *fuck you* officer, pulling me over on expired tags, I mean I was only two days late dawg....

Sutherland shadows them near the bar, hoping for a messy altercation. He turns away to suck on his inhaler and misses an underage patron maundering the tables for unclaimed tips.

The clock pops to three, Saturday night's heaviest hour. Romeo is launching into grins now as he makes clear headway with the ballet dancer.

— It was $225 a week with the company, I only got corps work, she says, one slender hand modestly pinching together the lapels of his jacket. I make that a night now. Exotic dancers have longer careers, too.

— You are absolutely right, Romeo agrees.

She opens the jacket and lifts a breast to show him a pink scar from where she had paid to have a size reduction to meet the demand of an art she later abandoned. Now she was saving to have them enlarged.

— More money in a bigger size, she says, and again, Romeo, fascinated, replies:

— You are absolutely right.

The dancer appears now to fully observe Romeo for the first time, to actually consider him as a real person and not a vague figure from a daydream, and the first hint of a smile tightens the soft corners of her mouth. She offers him her hand and says:

— Anantha. Anantha Bliss.

— What kind of name is that? Anantha Bliss?

— Not my real one.

Romeo's grin moves beyond his usual leer, and he takes her hand between both palms and raises all three hands together, a gentler version of his gentlemen's handshake. He has no idea what sort of transformation has just been introduced into his life, and as yet feels overwhelmingly confident.

Son of a bitch!

Those circled nearby turn and look; the corn-yellow teeth of Hellzapoppin's companion are bared in response to an unanticipated slap. He was feeling his whisky. Magically a compact mirror appears in hand and she adjusts herself accordingly, inspects her face for visible damage. Finding nothing permanent, she sneers at those who stare: *What're you looking at?*

On a run to the bathroom Romeo stops long enough to scoff at Sutherland's dutiful public stance (arms crossed over massive chest, feet shoulder-width apart, an air of smug alertness though his eyes appear aimed above the crowd at the far wall). He expresses sympathy for Sutherland's frustrations at being allowed only to watch.

— Big healthy boy like you and nothing to do but spectate? And we got crimes going down right now all over the neighborhood, some damsel in distress you can't do anything about!

Sutherland shoots a sullen stare. Since his suspension he has muttered this outrage often – that while he wastes time among the drunks at the Don Quixote there are *real crimes* being committed throughout the district. Like today's bus accident. What if a cop had been out there on a beat? The injustice just baffles him. But he doesn't mind a little play here and there with Díaz, and he refuses to take the bait the man has tossed him. He suggests Romeo had better be careful not to take too much time with the young boys in the bathroom, he might lose his girl to an off-duty cop.

— Off-duty is what you call it? Romeo laughs.

Sutherland ignores the question, happy with his picture of Romeo in action in the bathroom stalls.

— You probably wouldn't care about losing the girl if it meant you got to keep the boys, would you Díaz? he asks.

— Only man to suck me off was a cop like you. Except he was working.

The exchange heats quickly between these two men who never liked one another and never pretended to. Sutherland follows Romeo into the bathroom (the two stalls empty), questioning aloud Romeo's problems with authority, his macho spic bravado, his loneliness.

Back in the parlor Beau listens to their yelling and shakes his head, shrugs.

— I'm tired, he tells Glenda. Honestly I don't know how much longer I can stand this shit, it gets harder every night.

One hears such declarations from Beau on a regular basis.

Sparks ignite between HELLZAPOPPIN and his girlfriend, trading half-slaps and hard poking fingers as their companions scoot their chairs from the table with a weary, accustomed air. Haycraft, nearby and alone among it all deep in a book, raises his head and exclaims, *People, please!* but they ignore him. He scans unsuccessfully for Chesley Sutherland. Beau is of no help, either, a frantic blur behind the bar now as the redneck boys high-five one another, backing hard into other guests.

HELLZAPOPPIN clutches his girlfriend's hair in his fist, and Haycraft raises to his full height. *Dear people, I insist,* he begins, just as Romeo stumbles rumple-shirted down the steps to the bar, shouting that he wants Beau's aluminum baseball bat. The dancer smiles and rolls her neck on her shoulders, the jacket falling open. She is leaving. Sutherland smiles to her as he gambols out of the bathroom beaming, sliding a raw-ham hand over his stubbled head. He is bumped shoulder to shoulder by a man skipping out on his tip, a surprise so impudent and unthinkable that Chesley can only stand still and watch him follow Anantha Bliss out the door. And at the height of it all slings the wild clanging of a brass bell, Beau's hand desperately yanking the hammer rope, and the tension washes up in the air with the ceiling fans, vanishing into Beau's punchline cheer: *Time to tilt at the windmills, folks!*

Outside it is morning. The night is now over, its teeth marks still scraped across the sky.

HAYCRAFT
KEEBLER,
HUMMING

HAYCRAFT AWOKE BEFORE NOON
and fried up a breakfast platter of potatoes on a crusty hotplate, adding apple juice in a fogged wine glass culled from the clean side of a steel sink. As he took his breakfast Haycraft fetched his thoughts, hopeful it would be one of those fugitive hours when the thoughts would come. He considered himself "a man of dialogue," citing Plato's discourses as the prime example, and in these mornings the dialogues took place within himself – or at least *by* himself, in that he ranted around the cramped room, index finger pointed and raised, or hands turned out in muddled exasperation, head shaking as he voiced a multitude of questions (one giving rise to another) and, less often, answers to them.

Several points of view clamored in his head; he believed his particular genius lay in that he allowed himself to hear out each one. He often referred to his mind as the House of Representatives. If the dialogues would not come, he forced them to the surface via another fastidious protocol, his single obsessive hygienic rite: trimming his toenails. Haycraft Keebler had large feet with nails of maniacal growth. They required constant trimming and shaping, or else turned ingrown and disturbed his canvassing ambitions. He believed healthy feet formed the man: *If the feet are distressed, then so the soul.* Cryptically, he quoted Emerson: *We see with the feet.* Somehow this action with the clippers and file opened his inspirational well, acting as sergeant-at-arms to call his House to order.

After soaking one foot at a time in a large steel mixing bowl filled with steaming, salted water, Hay positioned himself on the single chair in his room, an old elementary-school chair with adjustable pressboard desk, which he reconciled so that one heavy foot rested upon it within his vision and also before the long double-hung window that gave onto the wide avenue outside. Snip-snip and click, then turning the file to smooth the newly exposed ridge, always perfecting each toe in turn rather than the sweeping gesture of cutting all nails across the foot before starting over again with the file. Murmuring as he worked: *It's in the details, boys, always in the tiniest details...* until the words fell way to a melodious hum of Stephen Foster or Broadway standards. He did not bother with the rinds spun onto the floor. His eyes centered upon the window and the street scene outside, or else the curtain of his mind's eye opened upon a loaded memory: an old woman pushing her belongings in a grocery cart rendered ruminations on why the city had a home for battered women but no shelter for the homeless specific to women (*their nightly risks must be enormous!*); an eight-year-old running about midday underscored the result of budgetary cuts from the truancy division of the police force; two men scrubbing away the spray-painted *faggots* from their doorway inspired his most high-profile success of helping usher through a fairness ordinance through the Board of Aldermen. Or, if not *actually* ushering that ordinance, he had at least helped in bringing the matter to some attention.

Everyone had a hard road, Haycraft knew. *But you have to start with the small, concrete details. Can't afford the broad gestures of historical perspectives – because that makes a question all or nothing, and absolute failure is not a possibility you can afford to entertain.* His father used to tell him that. His father, whom Hay remembered as an amalgam of Thomas Jefferson, Merlin, and the apostle Paul.

So Haycraft concerned himself with general issues but strained toward specific, practical steps. What bothered Hay in general was the disappearing middle class, the widening gap between the very rich and the very poor. He also found the local police force unnecessarily brutal and intimidating. In moments of lucidity he realized there was little he could do about these aside from pointing out the obvious to those who could hear him, and he accepted as likely that his commitment to these issues was mere cover to a deeper loneliness inside himself.... Alone and obscure, he responded by loving everyone in the abstract. But what bothered him in particular, in the details of daily life (and therefore actionable), was the debris that saturated Old Towne like a wild fungus ravaging a tropical village: He could see it from his school chair by the window, he stepped over it any time his schedule thrust him into the streets – the discarded junk, cars on cement blocks, engines in the alleyways, carpentry materials, old roof tiles, gutted fixtures and cracked moldings and furniture, asbestos lining, and refrigerators with still-attached doors ready to coffin some unsuspecting playful child. All this and more, uncollected. Here, in the district that displayed awesome examples of America's domestic architecture. Such sights wore on Haycraft; they inspired him. It was all going to change. Forcing a public bus to crash was merely an initial, active step.

Perhaps too firm of a step. He did hope the lady he had heard about was all right. He had been looking for an evocative statement, not an act of terror; he was an idea man.

Such ideas found their way into the broadside newsletter that he wrote, typed, edited, printed, and distributed himself: *The*

Old Towne Fair Dealer, on-time delivery of which he guaranteed and accomplished along with his voter registration routes, the words of the newsletter gaining an extra air of authority through their proximity to official documents. Other copies made their way under the windshield wipers of parked cars or met pedestrians face-to-face from telephone poles, or skittered down the street on the wind, clinging to pantlegs.

— Madam, would you care to take a moment to learn of our mayoral race and its dire implications on the course of your life, he would say to a scrawny figure in giant sports T-shirt and curls, clutching one infant and flanked on either side by wide-eyed and silent dirty-faced urchins, figures from Dickens transported to the city Hay had taken upon himself to redeem.

Grasping the mother's attention, he launched into his most laden rhetoric – a style ingrained from his father's campaigning days, when Haycraft himself had been the plump-cheeked child clutching the trouser leg, the difference being that *this* leg had been clothed in worsted wool, and that Hay's face as a child had been clean, spit-shined by his mother's kerchief, his hair brilliantined, his teeth white, his tongue stinging from a drop of cachou. His discourse threatened unholy annihilation by the indifferent powers-that-be of the lowly citizen doing her best to make ends meet. Once this fear had been staked precisely in heart, Hay's *Fair Dealer* appeared among the registration forms – forms he filled out himself in order to trouble the potential voter as little as possible, asking for signature only, sometimes signing for them beside their X.

UTILITY CREWS IGNORE OLD TOWNE STORM DAMAGE. PLASTICS TOOL & DIE: CITY ATTEMPT TO POISON OUR CHILDREN? From declining library funds to sewage anxieties to the rise in teenage prostitution and the latest police brutality; from calls for a civil review board to the syringe recycling program, Haycraft's House of Representatives covered them all. *Smothered and covered them all*, he liked to say, with each article subtly steeped in his avowed subtext, his final goal: nothing less than full secession of the district from the city of Montreux. *Old Towne as autonomous community.* Haycraft Keebler, political philosopher and populist idealist, manic-depressive man-about-town, was a secretly subversive character.

And who could not believe him? Who in such a lost and forlorn community could not be left with the suspicion that this charismatic and feverish man at the doorstep was not *on to something?*

Away with apathy! he shouted, striding through the alleyways. *You are not so content! If our souls are on their knees, then let us bleach clean the pavement!* Haycraft believed the people's indifference only masked their fear, and that this fear was little more than a child's staring at a lake, not yet knowing how to swim.

He embodied enough outward signs of the kook to prove convincing: ski cap in summer, pin-striped trousers held by buckled suspenders; massive feet bursting at the seams of plastic sandals – sandals he vehemently defended as necessity, for their massaging fibers allowed his head to remain clear and focused, and his odd widths and low arches made it difficult to find good, proper-fitting shoes. A polo shirt buttoned to the neck still could not hide the splash of hair graying over the collar, curling to the loose, stippled skin of the neck and chin, scarred with red streaks from years of poorly prepared shaving (he shaved using the same steel bowl where he soaked his feet, and prepared his skin with a bar of castile soap). Clean-cut but cursed with oily hair, all six-feet-two and 220 pounds of him rooted in your doorway, the glint of passion in reserve cornering his eyes and you, tired from a hangover that has lasted into its third day or jonesing hard for a cigarette since you swore to quit (or at least cut back) instead of paying that new tax of seventy-five cents per pack, sickly full with beans and eggs for the umpteenth time, anxious over your station in life or else not giving a shit at all – your lack of a job or even direction crushing your blunted senses, and what's this you hear about your benefits being cut off soon, and why won't the kids shut up, and was that neighbor boy in the stolen SUV backed onto a fence post really trying to run over those police officers so that they had to shoot and kill him with sixty-four rounds? – and you, weighted with this day of your life in arrears, find this strangely focused but intensely assuring bear of a man in your doorway, unbidden, telling you that with the least bit of effort on your own part, with support from himself and his streamlined network of volunteer agents, this life of yours can change. *For the better.* For the problems you face are not yours alone, but the entire community's. And that community is ready to act. All you have to do is sign here (or allow him to sign for you), join this mailing list, perhaps answer your phone if you have one. Endeavors will soon be undertaken.

Why not? What do you have to lose? He's not preaching the glories of freshly minted religion; he's not even asking for a hand-out. Here was a man with a mouth perpetually formed to say *yes*. Here was a man who spoke of practicalities. And he wanted to do all the work himself. Why not?

Naturally not everyone was pleased to find hulking Keebler at the stoop of their home. Those who lived in the few blocks of restored mansions (trapped, like Beau and Glenda, by the *Come Back to Montreux!* campaign) could do without him. Desperately hip young lawyers and fund-for-the-arts economic developers and anti-Freudian existential psychoanalysts and the entire fey interior-design fetishists crowd preferred to keep to themselves behind gilded walls and sculpted cornices, protected by brick and iron barriers. Haycraft could not access many of them due to the elaborate security systems at their gates; others owned vicious canine defenders, an animal Haycraft held a nearly superstitious fear of. So he steered clear of these homes by habit (discreetly rolling a copy of his broadside and dropping it through the iron bars), although he was not afraid to approach these owners for brief recruitment talks should he find them offhand some evening in the Don Q, dining on one of Glenda's homemade spanikopitas or drop biscuits. But Beau did not want Haycraft pestering the ostensibly well-heeled patrons, that sacred few. Credit-card charges zoomed directly to his bank account, but the ratio between checks cleared and checks written was always a precarious one for the Stileses.

It was the lower castes of the Old Towne citizenry that gave Hay his heroic impulses and adamant fervor; they were the ones who most needed the catalytic spark, the symbol of some martyr.... The educated near-rich he held no sway with and knew it – he approached their doors out of a sense of duty, not confidence; he stuttered and fretted and accomplished little if someone answered their door to his surprise. But The Lost, as he called them, inspired his obstinacy. With them he sought connection. The Lost had been his father's territory – to his father the lost and the local amounted to one and the same thing. *All politics is local, and the locals is lost,* he had liked to smirk when playing at his homespun manner, often, to his young son. So it was not beyond the realms of possibility that when Haycraft crossed paths with a particularly fragile soul, he might see the meeting as nothing less than the end of his solitary ways. A savior's life is a lonely one.

Haycraft came marching past empty playgrounds and vacant lots through a warren of rookeries, full of himself for having signed a new subscriber to his newsletter, a silk-hatted young man in a T-shirt inscribed with the maxim TATTOOS WILL GET YOU LAID. They had agreed that if his secession plans succeeded then Hay could promise the young man a place in his cabinet, or at least a position in the cabal or shadow government he expected to organize to unofficially run things. On that glorious October day of ecstatic light sinking on the crisping leaves and cigarette butts he crushed under sandaled feet, shreds of burnt tobacco streaking behind his heels, Haycraft hurried to stay on schedule (the modest summit meeting had forced an extension to his allotted hours), until he was struck still with the same intensity as Jesus realizing sight of his first disciple.

Lambret Dellinger was the vision. Just a boy, fifteen and spindly thin beneath a white cotton Tee and faded black jeans, a pair of scruffy Doc Martens lifted from a thrift store covering his feet. He sat huddled beneath the glass wicket in the back gate at the Don Quixote, where the alley gave way to a stone garden Glenda tended, fenced in by fraying, treated wood. His hair was so black it appeared nearly blue in the shade, spiraling coils falling over his dark brown eyes and soft pale cheeks that were each rouged by the coming evening chill. He had never shaven, had never needed to. He sat with his back to the fence, arms crossed over the knees, chin on wrists, eyes staring blankly through waves of sheened hair. Absently he rolled a length of iron pipe back and forth along the length of his foot, the metal singing a sharp note about him. The stink of the city sifted in the alley breeze.

Haycraft, unaccountably bereft, beheld him. So taken by the sight he did not even notice car parts freshly dumped the length of the alleyway, nor the rolled chain-link fencing coiled against the curb. He shifted his satchel higher on his shoulder, transposed his weight from one hip to another. It was no good, he could not speak. He moved the satchel from right shoulder to left, waiting, his mind an empty slate, his eyes enlarging at the prospect of the boy – a mere wastrel! – descried there, he felt certain, *as a sign*: a sign for Haycraft only. Alone and bursting with youthful life – the violet splotches beneath his eyes notwithstanding, nor the stink of the rag soaked with mineral spirits drying between his wrists – a portrait of raw elegance in repose. His hair, wild and abundant, fell in thick locks over a surprisingly serene forehead. Surely the boy knew Haycraft was there, gazing haplessly. Why didn't he say something? Then again, why didn't Haycraft speak? For hours each day, unrestrained speech sprung from Hay's tongue to total strangers. Now it was no good. His thoughts crossed and recrossed and crisscrossed the paths of his mind, retracing his history of ebullient and confident conversation, his witticisms, his implications, his clever asides and jocularities. He found little help. Only one offering came to his veering mind:

— Hello? Haycraft asked.

Met with silence. The autumn breeze came again, more forcefully now, shushing wrappers along the cracked tar and unmoored cobblestones; the sun's brassy light pulled along the backs of the houses with it. The boy stared straight ahead, his limp gaze fogged in such unusual light, vaporous, lacking focus. The metal pipe sung out its single steely pitch.

— Hello? Haycraft asked again, emboldened by the boy's silence, as though such silence suggested vulnerability, a plea for aid. This time his voice registered on the boy's face; the heavy eyelids blinked slowly, the head moved with a deliberate and indulgent roll of the neck. His round cherub's chin lifted briefly from his arms. The rag fell free to the ground then, presenting Hay with the only blemish to that perfect face: a cloud of raw, pink skin flamed about the mouth. The boy lay his head back against the wood planks behind him, lazily – *demurely*, Haycraft would describe it later – and the eyes, glowing with a micalike shine, took the man in.

— Hello boy, Haycraft said yet again, a final time.

The boy answered with his own hello, after a good long pause, apparently forced to go some lengths in search of the word.

He speaks! bellowed Hay. The words came rushing then. Such a handsome and able-bodied young boy, Haycraft said, and here he sits alone? Why, did you have a fight with the parents? I'm not sure I understand what you mean by *no parents*. Everyone must come from someone, I don't believe things have changed that much since I was your age. How difficult the young must have it these days if what you tell me is so. What do you mean, you are working? But working how, crouched like this in one of our unfortunate alleyways, when it should be the world crouched before you, crouched at your feet! No, I do not lie!

Tell me, have you eaten? Would you like me to give you, boy, something to eat?

Lambret sneered, he mumbled almost incoherently in a soft and broken voice; it would cost the man twenty-five dollars.

Such an exchange made no sense to Haycraft.

— What's that? You would charge me for the gift of giving you nourishment?

The boy's eyes crimped as though taken in sudden headache. The chin fell firmly down to his arms again. He worked his lips between his teeth, stretching the irritated skin around them.

— Come on now, I don't have the entire evening. I am behind schedule as it is, and you see it is very important to stick to a plan as it was designed, mmmhmmm. Let's get you a good cheese-burger. Glenda makes the best in town and uses only the leanest meat available and buys only from farmers who do not employ growth hormones, and with his hand reaching from beneath the satchelled shoulder he waited. He waited, and wondered, looking over the boy, thinking *What have I found here, just look at the sight of him, a prince unanointed,* as Lambret asked if a cheeseburger was really all he wanted to give him, his eyes gathering focus now. He took to his feet slowly, slovenly. He admitted he could stand something to eat all right.

All thoughts of The People and The Lost, of land co-ops and entrepreneurship programs and the need to beautify these alleys and to draw patrons to the pleasures of the Don Quixote, disappeared before the prospect of the boy Lambret Dellinger. It would be getting to night soon – Hay could feel the shifting hour like the edge of a blade to his ribs – and there Haycraft was, stuck outside, and so far off schedule that he was humming again, his first hint of agitation. The lengths of his nerves fluttered alive with hummingbird wings. Usually a case of worry. Yet the Don Q was only a few steps away, and twilight had arrived – the hour that always led him to recall the Tennessee farm his family had fled to; when the peacocks leapt to the low branches and screeched their mournful cries; when Haycraft had no concerns further than finishing the nearest book at hand, and arriving home in time for dinner, and the parlor games invented by his parents. It would be night soon, yes, which meant time to allow the day's duties to slide into memory and to relax one's way-worn body among fellow strivers and comrades. The nights at the Don Quixote always did evoke in Haycraft the feeling of a reward bestowed.

§

— Look what I've found, Haycraft announced to the regulars upon entry, setting down his satchel on his corner table before approaching an open barstool nearby. A new friend recruited to our aid, plucked right off the street. And hungry, too.

Beau Stiles smiled down to the curiously young face. No doubt he made up his mind in that instant as to Lambret's condition, station, and the level of surveillance he would require. Beau had the gift of making snap judgments of character while his face betrayed nothing more than considerate attention. He moved the tip jar marked HAY'S RENT outside of Lambret's reach as he asked the boy what he might like to eat.

— One of Glenda's famous cheeseburgers, Haycraft said. I promised him already.

The rest of the regulars offered a cautious welcoming as a family takes in a stray dog, undecided on whether it could stay for fear it might be rabid, dying, or belong to someone else. They were willing to keep it fed for the moment, willing to grant the stray a pat on the head. Haycraft had invited in The Lost before. Usually these were yammering bag ladies of the grocery-cart variety, rag-arrayed beneath plastic head covers, the dour and dowdy aged who swooned in sleep at the comfort of a booth and whistled through piano-board mouths, leaving Beau and Glenda to wonder what to do.

Lambret didn't mind the new faces, the interior decor strangely foreign and otherworldly (all that stained wood, the palms and brick, the hanging paper lamps) filtering through the easy fumes in his head. Happy chance had placed him there, though once darkness fell fully over the city with its shroud of safety, he would need to slide out onto the streets again to Frederick Park. But that would be later. A boy on his own: Lambret was in no position to complain about any help he might stumble upon.

The adults observed Lambret closely, searching for clues in whether he ate his fries by hand or by fork (he ate them by hand), and with what manner he approached the cheeseburger. Lambret tore at the sandwich; he ate with a voracious appetite. That pleased Glenda, who prepared all the food from scratch, using her mother's basic recipes and channeling her father's improvisatory panache to make the dishes her own. She was especially proud of her cheese-and-garlic-crammed drop biscuits, and was happy to see that she did not have to force the boy to try them. Moreover, she had not seen her own son since he left for college on a partial scholarship in drama nearly a year before, and so was gratified to speak with a boy not too far from his age. For the recognition; for the memories of her own house once filled with all kinds of loud, rumbustious teenage boys.

The over-twenty-one policy didn't take hold until nine o'clock. As Lambret sucked down soda after soda, Glenda plied him with questions about schoolwork and family, questions he evaded with shrugs and the phrases *it's okay* and *they're all right*, evasions that did not bother her (he was a teenager after all), as his silences allowed her to relate stories of her own son, Damon, and the letters he wrote home from Texas, and her worries over the loans he had taken to get by *in such a large state as Texas*, she said; how could a drama major ever expect to pay off his loans?

— Something about being a Stiles, we're just built for debt

I guess, she fussed, gesturing at the bird's-eye maple wood trim on the backbar, the mahogany of the bar itself.

— But he does love his education, she continued. At least he does now. I wonder how he'll feel when the bills come due and he's working steakhouse theater.

— Or a girl turns his head, Beau added, smiling.

Glenda laughed with delight. It was a shared joke having to do with their own history, though they never let the regulars in on the exact reference.

— He never responds to my letters, grumbled Haycraft.

— You don't write him letters, Hay, you send off your news-letters, Glenda answered.

— Yet each is a personal missive from me, directed to any individual whose eyes might grace my four humble pages. My thoughts and observations, things I want the boy to respond to! Simply because I don't scribble *Dear Damon* at the top or sign off with my fondest wishes doesn't mean I don't want to hear from him. It is important – of utmost importance – to stay in touch with the views of the young. *To nurture.* They have a much clearer perspective on our society than we, who are hopelessly enmeshed within it....

Maybe such proclamations best accounted for Haycraft's initial attachment to Lambret: the man's desire to stay in touch with the young. Many times before he had voiced his attraction to all things of energy and beauty, and despite a sulky temperament under the influence of inhalants, the boy provided a good deal of both. Once the effects of his habit wore off, Lambret was bright, questioning, the eyes no longer glazed, but large and curious. He showed a compassionate heart in caring for a number of stray dogs collected from the neighborhood, sheltering them in the wreck of an abandoned house off one back alley, nursing the injured ones – such as Blind Mooch, who had been blinded by a rat – back to health. He played crate basketball with other kids, or else sat out the midnight hours with a spray can in hand to sketch his tag on any surface he deemed appropriate.

But for money he worked a walk in Frederick Park, the shuffle line of urgent, shadowy men who crept past the statue of Haycraft's father with one hand on their money. Any one of them there at the bar could guess at what he did on first sight: The initial glance required a doubletake to clarify whether he was boy or girl. He appeared to be in-between. Despite soft features, his face betrayed a lean hardness advanced for someone so young – it betrayed a life accustomed to sleeping in the odd spot, the dark stairwell or dried culvert, his face. Haycraft seemed happy, but what could a hustling boy want from him that was any good? When the two arrived again at the exact same time the next evening, suggesting the youth was not going to disappear at once (that Haycraft's schedule had made a minute adjustment), the conclusion was apparent on the face of each one there: They would have to keep an eye on this Lambret kid. Haycraft was one of their own, after all.

§

There was nothing suspicious to find in their attachment, in Hay's point of view. Haycraft *gave*, so it was only natural that in turn he should attract a trustworthy, giving companion. And Lambret was as different from the other night-boys working the park as the drawing of a tree is different from a real one. They forged a bond partly on Lambret's love of graffiti – or, more precisely, his knowledge of and intimacy with the usefulness of spray paint and its variety of possible applications. Lambret could sing a rhapsody to the glories of spray paint, the pleasure found in the hiss of aerosol, the rattle of the ball in a quivered can, the comfortable fit to the grip of his hand, the satisfaction of instant surface transformation. Sensing a poetic strain in the boy for the first time, Haycraft encouraged him to describe his passion further; and, listening closely, head angled backward as he scratched softly at the raw flesh of his shaved neck, Hay's House of Representatives was called to order, wherein a lively debate commenced.

Because the contrivance of a bus wreck was not enough. Executed perfectly, it achieved nothing more than two newspaper articles detailing the event, and one self-righteous editorial condemning the sick minds of a few obscene souls. (A complete misreading, in Hay's view.) It turned out the woman he'd heard of had been only grazed by the fender, causing a few scrapes and bruises. The city hauled away the debris that caused the accident, and the event disappeared. The rest of Old Towne still suffered its crisis of uncollected refuse, especially in the forgotten alleyways – those passages Haycraft and Lambret both knew with the familiarity of lovers.

The city rarely flagged in regular collection of bagged trash; outside of the odd strike here and there by put-upon workers, curbside pickup occurred every Thursday. No, the crisis lay in the larger objects, the materials discarded by bankrupt manufacturers, tobacco rollers, abandoned construction sites, the fled well-to-do: culvert pipes, random iron and metal scrap, ancient air conditioners and ovens, railroad materials left over from the historic Nashville line (which cleaved the district, but not as definitively as the affluent would have preferred). Even distaffed telephone poles remained strewn over the original paving stones, clogging the narrow passages that Haycraft utilized in his canvassing endeavors; passages that Lambret and his pals used as escape routes from the likes of the Chesley Sutherlands out there who were not serving suspension-with-pay. Lambret and his pals were large-scale graphomaniacs, surmised Haycraft. Trick money in hand (or, more commonly, with the discount secured by a jacket of ample pockets), they cleared

the hardware stores of acrylic spray paint and permanent
markers and then covered storefront security gates and street-
level power boxes, public telephones, bus stands, concrete
viaducts, newspaper dispensers – any workable surface on
which a kid could stamp his tag. What was left in the cans and
markers flowed through the boys' nasal passages, a practice
Haycraft abhorred instinctively, disgusted by the sight of their
soft mouths circled by inflamed haloes, peppered acne, flakes of
paint. He went about them thrusting his handkerchief to their
faces, often spitting into the cloth first like a mother scrubbing
her child on the steps before church. A practice that set off the
boys into bursts of embarrassed laughter. A sound Hay liked.

But first things first: At this time Haycraft was much more
concerned with the graffiti the boys practiced than with their
health. Before Lambret, he thought the wild looping caricatures
and obscure tags an irritant to the urban eye; but once he had
met, and watched, and listened to Lambret passing time with his
friends, throwing bones or watching the dogs wander through
empty lots, he grasped *graffiti as possibility*. With Lambret in
mind, the unintelligible scrawls became not a further junking of
civic culture but a legitimate form of underground expression. If
nothing else (Hay maintained to Beau and the scattered regulars
at the sunken bar, over several wet autumn days), the images
brought attention to those objects usually ignored.

— A power box; the back of a stop sign. It's as though you've
never seen them before. Suddenly there they are, singular and
credible, worthy of scrutiny.

Romeo Díaz snorted at what he considered to be another in a
long line of Hay's "inane" campaigns – crusades he believed
came only to a man who had the leisure to imagine them and
who, he would say, approached reality *at the most present angle of
convenience*. He toasted Haycraft's new insight with Dewar's and
soda; he asked Hay if the kid had introduced him yet to the

aerosol can's other recreational uses. But the notion of graffiti as environmental enhancement outraged Chesley Sutherland.

— There's nothing singular about it! *Incredible* is the only word I have for the contempt these kids show – it's arrogance pure and simple, covering our public works like kudzu. They are defacing public property, Hay, doesn't that bother you?

Chesley had his ideas, too; *Sutherland's Laws*, they called them. He preferred "The Sutherland View." *If you want to hear the Sutherland View on the problem,* he might begin, entering a conversation on capital punishment, *I say you dust off the chair and plug it back in.* His main tenet being that actions against his sense of the public good must be met with an opposite and overwhelming reaction, for example, any kid caught at the bus station with spray can in hand should be prosecuted to the full extent of the law.

— We don't have much to punish them with, he admitted. But watch your pennies and the dollars will take care of themselves. Hit the kids hard for misdemeanors and then it's easier to nail them later at the felony level. 'Cause trash always comes back. Get them locked away soon and you never have to worry about them again.

Haycraft rarely digested the opposing thoughts of others. Usually disagreements led only to his further fastening of mind. The work of Lambret's cronies had raised Hay's awareness; innocuous objects no longer escaped his attention, and surely he wasn't alone in such sudden insight. Despite intense efforts he had never succeeded in bringing attention to or engineering the erasure of Old Towne's alley debris. Therefore, cover said debris in graffiti, and the necessary attention would be drawn.

Haycraft had the ideas, Lambret the ability. Their projected canvasses rarely consisted of flat surfaces, and Hay could hardly draw a coherent linc by hand, much less with a spray can. But in the way a poet tackles a devilish meter to express his thought and finds the restriction inspiring a more luminous work than would the endless freedom of blank verse, Haycraft discovered his vision in his absence of finesse. *Never miss the majestic villa hidden in the tight villanelle*, he quipped. He would undertake his project with a monochrome aesthetic: all surfaces laminated in gold.

He swore the boys to not indulge in any momentarily inspired, improvisational creations. The plan throbbed with such promise that he took the worrisome step of adjusting his daily schedule: First he consulted his calendar for the upcoming moon phase (the success of new projects required getting started before the new moon); he took the bus to a suburban hypermarket and filled a rolling suitcase with materials; then he arranged three twenty-two-minute meetings with the small band of aerosol guerrillas in his apartment. There he presented the boys with targets marked on a district map hung over the chipped plaster of his apartment wall and disastrously hand-drawn by Hay himself. Boys he had come to like, even admire, despite the sharp chemical stench. He surged into the awaiting room like water rushing from a burst main, overwhelming the boys in seconds. He sat with them on the couch with one large leg crossed in front like a railroad gate, curling his arm over the back to clutch a boy's shoulder, careful never to touch anyone above the knee for fear of alienating him. He drank water from the same glass of any boy he spoke to, thinking such earthiness persuasive. Over three short evenings Haycraft exulted in his hidden capabilities as a general, delineating missions for each group of three clad entirely in black, provoking them with fiery (but brief) motivational speeches before launching the lads out with his blessings, into the dark.

— It's true I ask you to take grave risks, Haycraft admitted. But remember the hand that builds is better than that which is built. *Better and nimbler than the hand is the thought which wrought through it*, as Emerson so rightly remarked.

The boys hardly understood him and did not care. They liked the idea of their work being somehow sanctioned, and here was an adult with a place of his own, a place where any or all of them were welcome to crash. They thought him nuts but cool, an easy touch.

Meanwhile Haycraft continued his scheduled forays to the Don Quixote, as a cover.

— In order to retain a sense of normalcy, he explained. To delay suspicion. This mission is illegal, I want you all aware of that. It must be dispatched in total secrecy. You are to be artful terrorists; harbingers of an awful beauty.

Haycraft was not interested in the threat of arrest. He believed civic disobedience should be anonymous, so that a government could never be certain how large a wave of unrest they were dealing with, thus leading them to suspect the worst. He believed in covert coercion.

The boys launched themselves out his door in giggling glee. Each night, Haycraft inspected their handiwork as he walked home from the Don Q, humming his light Foster tunes and smiling to himself at three in the morning, on schedule, the full moon still some days away. And he was happy to open his door upon the splayed form of Lambret each time, asleep on the covered couch beneath a dusty sheet, among another boy or two on the floor. He stepped lightly over the wagging tails of curled dogs, trying hard not to be frightened, and ignored the soiled rag in Lambret's hand.

Four nights' work and the task was done. *Mission accomplished*: Immediately the new artworks entered the conversation of the city; citizens began to take note of the lengths of pipe and rolls of wire mesh resplendent in gold beneath radiant sunlight. Snap judgments occurred on the merit of the works as art – usually asserting the negative – but the point was that the debris was now *noticed*. With outrage and an inward shudder, in most cases, and in these instances the Board of Aldermen passed motions to have the works removed. As had been planned and hoped for all along.

Added, unforeseen benefits were of consequence, too. A handful of the works were left to stand in the forsaken corners where the boys had mounted the debris in a kind of found-object sculpture, met with a puzzled shrug by the average Old Towne individual, few of whom claimed to have much insight into the baffling absurdities of Contemporary Art. High-res photographs appeared in *Montreux Magazine* and in the new color editions of the newspaper. There were discussions on the local talk radio, and brief investigations on the nightly news. Such small successes were only an added award in Haycraft's view. What mattered in the end was that the debris was gone, and his neighborhood's grand architectures now had the chance to breathe.

Haycraft was aware this achievement was due in large part to the abilities of the boy.

At the Don Quixote, the regulars fells into ripe discussion. An operation on such a large neighborhood scale overthrew even baseball as a topic of debate; the world could have been covered in gold for the intensity with which they evaluated the act. Romeo stuck to his indifference – he kept his 1968 BMW out of the alleyways and the debris had never bothered him. Beau Stiles said he liked the spirit of the thing, though he wasn't sure he understood it. A grumbling Chesley Sutherland declared it still vandalism, and that if he were allowed to return to duty he would get the bastard kin who were at the bottom of it, rounding up all implicated by martial means. He said this with an eye cast at Haycraft, who everyone suspected had been secretly involved. Haycraft turned his palms upward, baffled by the attention.

— Always a crime somewhere, always some punk looking for an arrest, Sutherland muttered. And here I am stuck with you guys, making sure you don't hurt yourselves.

Just then Romeo Díaz raised his glass and launched into a mocking toast, christening Keebler *Our Napoleon in Rags*, a moniker Haycraft disparaged haughtily among the other regulars as insulting, but one that at home he quietly cherished, using the title to sign his notebooks.

— Although I've never appreciated the warlike spirit of any man, I have always admired the figure of Napoleon in history, Haycraft explained once, alone with Lambret. Emerson wrote a laudable essay about him, you know. He spoke of the man as a figure created by the people, by the times. Europe gave birth to Napoleon out of neccssity, and he rose to the demand. I cannot imagine a more noble call to heed.

§

Quietly the Don Q regulars came to tolerate the new presence of the boy in their cloistered world. Lambret's profession in the park was something of an open confidence – not that he hid anything by his low-slung black jeans, the loose, dirty T-shirts that hung on his lithe, nearly frail frame, and the pouting, helpless stare that seemed the default expression of his face. They tolerated him by not beating him to a pulp any time he followed Haycraft into the bar. But their uneasiness was palpable: No one could see what the boy could possibly want with a man like Hay that did not imply manipulation. As a ward of the state, Haycraft did have consistent money coming, and his family had provided a very small trust – Beau and Glenda concerned themselves with that possibility. Romeo disliked Lambret because of his sexual ambiguity; he detested such confusions on principle. He thought boys should be all boy, playful and destructive and ready to goof until the age came to get serious. (Whenever *that* was.) Chesley Sutherland thought the kid a punk who had lured Haycraft into pedophilia – a crime. He did not want to be forced to tip off his contacts on the force, but Chesley believed he had to do what he had to do.

What bothered them all, strangely, was apparent affection. Haycraft's hand calmly stroked the black, almost French curls of Lambret's hair; his palm rested easily on the thin neck as they gazed together at the television behind the bar. They leaned into one another in all occasions. They worked together closely – unusual work, too, with Lambret reading aloud from Thoreau and Emerson, and Haycraft interrupting to make a gentle corrective of pronunciation or else expand upon the writer's ideas. This sight eased Beau and Glenda's concerns a notch on their inner dials, but the regulars did not know what to make of it: They felt forced to watch the two incline their heads toward one another over a table, sharing a smile, a gentle touch, the pleased pucker of Haycraft's lips. Eccentricities of character were ably assimilated here; there is a kind of friendship where people appear ready to bare their teeth on the other's throat, and they continue like that all their lives yet never part. The Don Quixote was filled with such friendships; as Sutherland said, *Everyone here's fucked up some way or other.*

Now there they were, confronted by one of their own in the company of a fifteen-year-old boy.

— And not *all* boy at that, Romeo insisted. And he may not even be fifteen, I'm not convinced.

Chesley snickered. He told Romeo he sounded jealous.

— Maybe you need to get out to that park and get your own Lambret, man.

The idea held such promise to the suspended cop that he could not resist further extrapolating on the possibilities of what a Lambret could do for a lonely Romeo. Although Romeo could not afford such luxuries, Chesley added. He nudged Romeo with his elbow.

— What the guy needs is a woman, I'm telling you, Romeo

said, ignoring him. Someone who'll take care of *him,* not the other way around. I mean look at the kid: He's halfway to bitch already. I'm not convinced Hay's into male ass.

The others didn't respond. They continued to stare at the two in their booth, trying to act like they were not staring. Haycraft's sexuality had never been touched on in conversation before: It was not a subject worth pursuing; the guy was as sexual as a plant. So they thought.

They continued to watch and wonder as Lambret read aloud from a thick volume while Haycraft lounged, his head reclined on a pillow situated as a headrest behind the booth, his eyes closed in contentment.

— Maybe he plans to adopt him, Romeo ventured.

— I don't think that's the kind of daddy the kid is looking for, answered Chesley.

The two laughed a long time on that one. They were able to milk that one for weeks after, every night, any time the hours turned slow.

Beau thought such speculations hurt morale.

— You two hush up about that stuff, he said. I'm trying to sight the positive. That kid has a hard road and look at how Hay's getting him turned around.

— If I find Hay's getting it from the chicken here I'll take him down, I don't have a choice, Chesley spat.

— And I got a security camera showing you with a gun when you're not even on the force, Beau said.

— Not officially! Officially, I am not on the force. For now.

It was enough to shut Sutherland up. He needed Beau to vouch for his character at his deposition for reinstatement. Beau would do so, regardless of what Chesley did in the Don Q as long as it did not bring the place down – having a contact on the force can only help a nightclub owner in the long run.

§

If anyone would have thought to ask him, Lambret, after a good fumble for words, might have explained his relationship to Haycraft as similar to student and tutor. A charged relationship, yes, but when he thought over the details of their brief time together – Lambret was living in Haycraft's apartment within a few weeks of meeting him – he saw the older man teaching, himself doing his best with addled mind to listen. He was a boy in a hurry to grow out of childhood, and Haycraft opened the gate to a region reserved only for adults. It did not matter that these adults did not like or trust him; Haycraft assured him that eventually they would. And despite his velocity toward adulthood, Lambret still needed the example of an older man, however bent and tattered the model may be.

Haycraft gave the following explanation to Beau:

— He doesn't want my money, he never asks for anything. We read, and discuss, and I believe he is making great strides, then he disappears for days. He comes back, and I only need remind him of his father's example to set him straight for a while longer. His father was an adjunct professor, you know. Lambret mythologizes him, *the bewitched genius too close to the flame* sort of thing. That nonsense. But I'm slowly bringing him around to admit that the father is only an addict, that whatever gifts he may have had he let go for junk.

Haycraft had come to understand the powerful grip of the rags the boy carried, and his supply of aerosol cans, modeling glues; he had no use for the willful dulling of a mind. If Lambret preferred highs to the difficulties of concentration, Haycraft insisted he do it elsewhere. And often, the boy did. But always he came back, stray dogs panting in tow.

— Speaking of fathers, Hay, doesn't it bother you where he does his business? That's Edmund Keebler's statue they pass around. I would think that would bother you.

— My father is not watching, Beau. That statue is not my father.

What Haycraft would have liked to have said is: *What business is it of yours?* What if, when the boy arrived in early morning, considerate of the time so as not to disturb Hay's schedule, what if Haycraft opened his door to find Lambret standing alone, his face downcast, his fatigued eyes confessing to how absolutely lost he felt? What if Hay allowed the boy inside, and as he scolded him over his lack of hygiene, began to run the bath? If Haycraft then watched the boy undress and crouch into the tub, then kneeled there beside him, sponge and soap in hand; if he set to agitated humming while he lathered the boy's soft skin and saw the white flesh redden with the hot water; if he then dried the boy himself in the thickest towel he could find before leading him to the bed to rest. And if Haycraft decided to rest then, too – what of it? If Lambret stretched his thin body long across the coverlet and let his towel fall aside, lying quietly while Haycraft traced shaking fingers the length of his legs, his back, the line of his jaw – was it anyone else's concern? The boy had been providing himself long enough to have forgotten safety; he was as stubborn and clever as Copperfield without any of that character's charming innocence. Haycraft saw his ministrations toward the boy as acts of cleansing – washing away the street, the chemicals; washing away the ignorance from the urchin's mind. Haycraft wanted to gather the Don Q crowd before him and shout: I *am not Mather Williams' cousin dragging the boy behind a dumpster, steak knife in hand.* He was convinced that Lambret, his discovery, had no one but him, and Haycraft's very being was composed of an irascible need to save *some*one.

It was Glenda who finally mustered enough courage for a direct interrogation. Haycraft gave away nothing:

— We teach each other, he said. It's very much in the spirit of the Ancient Greeks: I give of my learning, and in turn he gives of his goodness and his will to learn. An eye-opening proposition for me, as I'm sure it would be for you also, Glenda. Like being allowed a glimpse of the future. Lambret has both man and woman in him; he embraces both, both archetypes. That is the way of the future, and I want to understand it.

Glenda smiled. She could display an accommodating smile, one that pinched the corners of her mouth and stretched the thin mauve strips of her unpainted lips, but which had no effect on her eyes. Her eyes remained steady, the flesh about them loose and puckered, thick, soft. It was a smile that said *take your time* when waiting for a patron's order, exhibiting infinite patience even at those moments when she had none.

— Yes, very much like the Greeks, or the Romans, Haycraft continued, rolling now. Don't you see how this folds into all my other endeavors? We read together as in Augustine's time, when reading was communal and our modern notion of tackling a book in solitude would be passing strange to society, when *to read* meant *to listen*; to own a book was to memorize it for recitation – note this down, Lamb, here's a future editorial subject; perhaps we have become so cut off from one another in this age because of our approach to reading, the massive distribution of books for sale rather than a borrowing-in-common; certainly the isolation of television-watching has its impact in this too; yes, this is a thought worthy of pursuit, it fingers everything....

— Yes that's all very nice Hay, but remember Beau and I aren't running a public library here and your friend is very young in the eyes of the outside world, chided Glenda. I'm asking you to keep in mind our situation.

— Yes, yes, of course, I understand. But *you* must understand that there is something so appealingly vague about him, like holding a memory, a comforting and nostalgic memory.

— The memory I have is coming to see you in the hospital, Glenda answered, covering Haycraft's hand with her own. She was referring to a time in Hay's twenties, when he had first become infatuated with another boy from the streets who ended up beating him when Haycraft refused to be more forthcoming with his money.

But Haycraft and Lambret were no longer following her. They were looking past Glenda, toward the half-wall that separated the dining room from the bar.

Mather Williams stood leaning over the handle of his broom, shoulders curled inward, hands folded over the top-most point of the handle as a bored king sits with his scepter, chin resting there, eyes in a bird-dog bead at Lambret. A kink in his head made him pounce upon a word just spoken and then launch into riffs from it: *Teaching the future, what do you think he mean by that. Teach him what, how to be a woman? Don't teach me about women, no sir, I teach him how to keep away from me.... I like women fine all right but that don't mean I want to be one, no sir....* All the while staring that unnerving, unrelenting glare he could fall into, the eyes sharply focused on a place indistinct to the rest (Glenda said his name once, sharply) and which was all the more disturbing for the size and fishlike glitter of his striking, globular eyes (Romeo called out to him from the opposite side, but Mather didn't respond); the stare would end only once the run of thought had expended its energy and dived beneath the surface of some placid, silent lake hidden inside him. As it refused to do now. After a brief pause, when it appeared he had finished speaking, he straightened himself, shrugged as from sleep, and suddenly slung the wooden broom through the air at their table.

— Mather! shouted Beau and Romeo at once.

Chesley started down the steps into the dining room, but Beau was already upon the man. *You get away from me, you don't touch me now I can fix it!* Mather cried, flailing his bony elbows against Beau's strong hands. *You want lessons boy I teach my own lessons* Mather shouted, pulling against the lock of Beau's grip as he struggled to get at the two – who still sat at their table, surprised into stillness. Glenda was there suddenly with him too, saying

Hush now, Mather, why did you do that, why did you throw that broom? in her most calming, quiet voice. Talk to me now, why would you do such a thing like that?

With one arm poled against his chest she kept Chesley Sutherland from getting any closer to the upset man.

— Beau do you want my help, Chesley asked, and hawked a cough.

— No, it's all right, Glenda answered for her husband, and it appeared to be true, for Mather just as abruptly as he'd begun had now stopped shouting, had stopped fighting. He shook his head and began to cry, telling them all that he was sorry, he didn't mean to make such a fuss.

The broom lay spiked in the cushions where they sat, the long handle a javelin stretched across the table and books. Lambret smiled at the books as he began to methodically pull them from beneath the broom and restack them again in his lap. Haycraft gave a short, nervous laugh. He reached across the table and fingered a long curl in Lambret's hair, threading the boy's attention back to the broom between them.

— Most likely a question of the man's dosage, Hay assured him. I am a great believer that every man has a form of mind, his own genius peculiar to himself. I make no claims to understand our Mather, but I do admire him. As everyone should! He takes things as they are and fits himself to them as best he can and yet he remains perfectly genuine.

— You should apologize, Mather, Glenda said in the same quiet singsong as before.

— No I'm sorry I don't want to, Mather answered.

Haycraft announced that there was no need for apologies; perhaps someone would care to take away the broom so that he could continue to do his business. Already he was flipping through one book to a specific chapter, his cheeks and nose warming to a red flush; Lambret's attention turned with the sound of the fluttering pages. The thick finger fell from the dark curls and to the opening line that he wanted the boy to read. Chesley Sutherland took the broom away from the table and returned it to the closet behind the bar, as Glenda led Mather to the back, through the saloon doors to the kitchen.

— Perfectly genuine, Haycraft repeated. As are you, Lambret, my little Lamb. . . .

THE
ARTIST
OF
DELUSIONS

ROMEO DÍAZ WAS AS DISGUSTED AS
he was amused. He listened to Haycraft expound his defenses of Lambret, listened to his theories of how the boy embodied "both masculine and feminine archetypes," and could not resist making a wisecrack to Chesley Sutherland that yes, Hay was right to compare his new relationship to what was common in the Roman Era, but Romeo would not have chosen that time's practice of reading as an example – the rites of passage for young soldiers kneeling before their exposed mentors, mouths open, seemed more apt. Sutherland clasped his hands together with glee, his lips wet with a slobbery chuckle: *damn straight, fuckin' A,* he said. Though he did not fully understand what Romeo was saying.

Characteristically Díaz was disgusted and amused by much in this life. Including himself and his own "crack of light between two darknesses," as he would put it, misquoting a famous Russian author. The barren life of Montreux especially repulsed him. He believed the city an inferior one, riven by provincialism and boredom. On an inspired day he would add the banal observation that Montreux typified the larger culture's obsession with creature comforts, celebrity, the pursuit of material satisfaction, and thus an inauthentic life. Although he would be quick to point out that he considered himself a part of that culture, a bottle thrown into the ocean filled with the same water that surrounded it. Romeo considered this thought somewhat redeeming.

— We are made by others, he would say. I contain multitudes just like anybody else.

Perhaps. But Romeo would not want to admit that he contained Haycraft Keebler. He considered them polar opposites: As Hay strove for a neighborly, self-sufficient community – what he would call a society built on the Feminine Principles of tenderness and compassion – Romeo's vision (so far as he had one) entailed every man for himself. Preferably every man for himself following the example of Romeo Díaz. Emphasis on *man*. He could not understand why more people were not like him, especially men, although he thought most men were in fact exactly like him, just not as honest. He believed in anarchy; in his own art of living; in the refusal to deny the reality of his experience. His conviction in these accounts had led him to a deep point in a personal hell, a masculine hell he indulged and examined every evening from his stool at the Don Quixote:

— My life is not *like* a nineteenth-century Russian novel. No, *I am* a fucking Russian novel.

Beau's curled brow pressed for a clearer explanation.

— The question is what to do, how to live, Romeo said. How to live without innocent eyes, yet in a way that fulfills my what-would-you-call-it. My *nature*, I guess.

Identifying that nature and then mapping its avenues to social connection had long proved elusive. The voiced Sutherland View was that Romeo needed nothing more than a consistent, reliable lay, with the freedom to be left alone afterward. Sutherland liked Romeo as a schoolyard bully likes his prey; in badgering him Chesley could look at Romeo and think, *At least I haven't slipped that far.* So he supported Romeo in those moments when they were not at one another's throats, as a bully protects his victim from other stalkers in order to keep the lunch money for himself.

— Guy your age, he's got to get his ashes hauled every now and then, man. How long has it been, Romeo?

— That is not your concern, and it is also not the case, said Romeo.

He was a man of varied history, our Romeo. If many pictured their lives as a meandering journey, Point A providing some logic to the arrival at Point B, then Romeo's life had been like scattered buckshot shattering a window, each shard of glass a flake of his fate. His father fled Cuba as an orphan through Operation Peter Pan, after the revolution; as a teenager he begat Romeo, left him with his name, and promptly disappeared. Which was entirely within his rights, Romeo maintained, angrily. He called his mother a waddling barrage of used Christian debris, although he loved her. She instilled in him the necessity of rigorous study in order to make it in the world, telling him never to forget he was half-spic and so would have to work "triple-hard" to get anywhere in this backward state. It was for her that he took on the loans to get through community college, issuing afterward a banker, a position for which he had no aptitude. A loan officer. He enjoyed this appointment thoroughly, as it allowed him an underhand opportunity to keep the progress of certain ethnicities in check. He disliked Asians mostly, and after being burned on a short number of home loans early in his career he declared all blacks with incomes below fifty-grand absolutely untrustworthy. Even his own Hispanic culture was suspect. Romeo professed respect in industry, in both the economic sense and as an attribution of character. He groused his Hispanic origins had neither.

Like Beau and Glenda, Romeo had been caught by the *Come Back to Montreux!* campaign. Warmed by the near-invisible mortgage rates, he took residence in one of the more palatial Gothic mansions that had reached a level of some repair. He installed his mother in an upstairs bedroom because *I liked to hear her struggles with the banister.* Once she died (a whistling heart that finally blew with full trumpet fanfare), and before his art-of-living revelation, Romeo said he was free *to follow my delusions*: Like Haycraft, Díaz was an organizer at heart, one of limited achievement despite that he bore the gift of handsome Latino features, a lithe elegance and sophistication in his movements, and a fine ability on the piano. What he did not have was resiliency or staying power; he burned out quickly. Also he could not hide his contempt for those he wanted to enjoin.

— I like the *idea* of humanity, he often said. I just dislike every-one I meet. That does not make me a misanthrope.

First he founded the Atheist Agenda. Its triumph lay in that he was able to recruit thirty-five dues-paying members nation-wide. Romeo's faith in atheism rivaled the fundamentalists in fervor – much to the consternation of Beau Stiles, who thought such arguments bad for morale in a bar whose regular scalawags were already down on their luck enough without having to worry about the eradication of their souls upon death. *I don't care what you think or believe Díaz but just hush up about it here*, Beau often cut in if Romeo got rolling. Still, it was his passion, and he was greatly annoyed that misdirected christers had usurped American history by suggesting the country's forefathers had been pious men:

— Jefferson, Washington, Franklin – name any one of them! Atheists to the last! he argued, loud enough to stir Haycraft from his books and force him to seek out a corner farther away.

His tenacity in the Atheist Agenda led to his firing from the bank. The group's initial project had been to label Faith a psychological disorder in the American Psych Association's DSM-IIIR. Their letter campaign shot missives to every organization from the APA to congressmen to every counseling office they could locate, with each letter created from the word processor on Romeo's office computer. He used the bank's stationery and letterhead to cut costs. Once the bank learned of the project they were apparently sponsoring, Díaz was without a job.

— A brief lapse in judgment, he explained. Or maybe subconscious sabotage, my interior voice urging me on to what I consciously could not yet admit.

Or, reasoning further:

— A perfect example of how backward this town is. Provincial to the core. Could you imagine anything more than a slapped hand if I'd been caught in, say, Chicago?

Shocked at first by the firing, within hours he did not care. Romeo had an innate gift for planning – results were mixed but the planning was stellar – and soon he was on to his next (his term) *fiasco*: a coffee house called The Anarchist Philosopher's Stone. Known to its few habitués as The Stone. It too was located in Old Towne, in the bowels of what had been a distillery until Prohibition, then a granary, then a storage facility for military ironworks during the Second World War, until finally it lay open-armed to vagabonds, for decades. He left the decor much as he found it. The original stamped-tin ceiling cast enough of a pall of class to satisfy him, and otherwise the building reeked of an Old World anarchist den, complete with oily floor, bad lighting, heavy wood benches and tables, and a general air of conspiracy. He set up a tiny stage with a single microphone and a PA system that screeched feedback, in an effort to encourage public debates – specifically harangues against the existence of God.

But in the three short years of The Stone's existence he was appalled to see that humming mike gradually usurped by the likes of folk singers and poets, coffee-house stereotypes with holistic philosophies and a penchant for deism who spoke of the need for dialogue between Montreux's segregated races.

Patrons took to scribbling marker on the walls, an action Romeo could appreciate, even encourage, but aside from the occasional absurd declaration – *Sweet Jesus! The Monkeys Are*

Loose! – the walls were streaked in pithy peace-and-wonder epigrams ranging from the likes of William Blake to John Lennon (*that crank!* Romeo fumed). Díaz could not scare away these miscreants no matter how dismal and unaccommodating he made his space; he went as far as hiring an unwashed and reeking Mather Williams for a time, rifling through the man's pockets to halve his Thorazine so that the poor soul began to mumble and shout at his broom and dishrags, convinced they were threatening him; his artworks became mere slashes of crayons framed by incoherent rants and weblike scribbles; he lashed out once at a professor who surprised him by touching his shoulder, shattering the academic's glasses. Such events thrilled Romeo, and only further endeared Mather to the poets. They invited him to their homes. They tried to keep him organically fed. They asked him to recite his songs.

Romeo refused to be outdone. He rustled the wounded homeless from the Christian mission and settled them with newspapers at various tables, believing the stench of these men with crisps of leaves in their beards would prevent the patchoulis from lingering. But they only brought the men organic treats and bought them coffee. They asked the men to share their stories. One couple even drove them to the gym as their guests, to shower.

Romeo could not figure it out. Why had they chosen his Stone as their chapel? He was purposefully rude; he refused to fulfill orders for anything aside from straight espresso or regular coffee, calling the mochas, cappucinos, and Americanos listed on his chalkboard wussy drafts. He insulted the men with their small pointy beards and wire-rimmed glasses, he was suggestive to the women in their flowing flower dresses and nonprocessed-sugar-indulged thighs, with their untreated hair, their neck tattoos and pierced tongues. Yet every morning when he unlocked the door he was awash in the scent of patchouli. They came and they thanked Romeo for providing a space to explore their ideas and to have a chance to connect. They told him he was a much-needed boon to the neighborhood.

— A complete and utter fiasco, Romeo muttered.

Worse (to his horror and dismay), he found himself strangely intrigued by one of the floral-skirted women. He actually *encouraged* Amanda, whom he first met at the Don Q. But she haunted The Stone. She used to dance ballet but was now paying her way to a political science degree by dancing nude at the nearby Primrose Flesh on the Go-Go. Amanda Beckham preferred to go by her stage name, Anantha Bliss; she was lovely in the transparent way strawberry blondes are delicately lovely; her smile was gentle and knowing yet her eyes lied innocence. Then she opened her mouth and let gush a flood of attitude. Anantha read what she called Sarcastic Decadent Poetry, a school she believed she had invented herself, composed entirely of insults against the men who paid to watch her dance.

Romeo was captivated. Despite that it was poetry, despite her attentive and respectful audience, he was in rapture at the mere sight of her, at the soft sound of her voice. He reeled at the composed air with which she approached the stage, at the first whisper of her tremulous voice describing defiant farts into a paying man's face, at the invented humiliations she prepared for those who believed they might take her home after her shift. In iambic, too.

A girl always open to accommodation, she moved in with Romeo to his Ruin within weeks of meeting him. The Ruin was what he called the house bought with money left over from the sale of his gothic mansion, a sale made to prevent defaulting on his loan and thus joining – in his own estimation – the contemptible exemplars of his race. The Ruin stood in on of the lapsed areas of the district, two blocks from the slaughterhouse and meat-packers, a past nest to squatters and bindlestiffs. A naked house; it lacked insulation, and cold air moved briskly through the reek of urine and damp sediment; the walls had been robbed of copper wiring long ago; rolled coal still lay stacked in the basement, settling a black dust over the bottom level. Holes gaped from the contours of the floors, the walls, the ceiling, surprising first-time visitors into careful step.

— So far I've managed only the bedroom, Romeo said, leading Anantha there.

He spoke the truth. The bedroom was embraced by three fine solid white walls, with another of exposed brick at the head of the bed. Romeo had refurnished the fireplace – shorn of its iron facade by salvagers some time before – with ceramic tile, ghosting the exposed brick opposite at a certain hour of sunlight. The ceiling smelled of new plaster and the blonde-washed pine blinds glowed. The rest of the house left Anantha speechless with horror.

— The wiring is almost finished. I think. I've got to get an inspector guy to check out what I've done, Romeo explained with a wince. But the possibilities are exciting, right? You can help me fix it up? You've got all kinds of ideas, yeah?

Anantha said she would be glad to help, and soon. Right away, in fact, starting with shoring up the lax stairwell that craned at angles remembered from childhood nightmares. She let it be known that his habit of leaving the outside cellar door open to local derelicts disconcerted her, too – reacting with a scream to the moans and wheezy laughter from below that first full night in her new home. A change could be made there, she thought.

Quickly, Romeo found himself again scandalized by his own actions: He acquiesced to the wishes of a lover, to ideas not his own. A day wasted at the hardware store and in his own incompetent handiwork, with the installation of a new lock-bolt eventually requiring an entirely new door by job's end. Still, he enjoyed the sense of accomplishment. He presented her this small renovation with the same grandeur as if he had bought her a new house altogether, and Anantha appeared gently satisfied. She could see he was trying.

Her contentment lasted only a few more hours, however. After a time of casually anxious glances at the new door and shining lock, and with more sudden noises at hours later than the moon in the sky, she confessed she did not feel any more safe than before.

They exchanged arguments. They parted and fumed alone. There was the night she stayed over with "a friend" Romeo did not know, a figure Anantha would not even disclose the sex of, leading Romeo to pass that evening before a foot-long row of emptied highball glasses at the Don Q. She came back; she left again. The couple endured a nonspeaking standoff that lasted five days, by the end of which Romeo was reduced and buckled, willing to capitulate to whatever Anantha asked. *Just tell me what you want,* he pleaded.

He crouched on one knee where she straddled a barstool. He had bought her favorite red wine (an Australian shiraz) and tried to display his best manners and propriety. As touched as she ever seemed to be, Anantha smiled down at him and said:

— Okay, you asked for ideas and I have one. I understand you. (*She understands me!* he exploded to Beau later, supplication alive in his eyes; the phrase meant everything to Romeo.) You have a conscience problem, she said. You have contempt for everyone, yet you provide a free home to strangers. It makes a twisted kind of sense, and in theory I can agree with this. But I want to know who is downstairs.

— What? Who? So you're saying we interview the guys.

Anantha shook her head and told him to let her finish. She repeated her demand that all vagrants be cleared from the cellar. Save one. *Who?* Romeo asked again. Anantha pointed to a slouching Mather Williams, who was quietly folding napkins beside Glenda behind the bar.

The choice would not surprise anyone who had bothered to pay attention over the past several weeks. Mather had unwittingly charmed Anantha.

Done! Romeo shouted and slapped down his palm. He knew Mather as well as anyone; meaning, he knew nothing about the man. Gratefully he took Mather aside and explained to him his new living arrangements, happy to welcome Anantha back to his Ruin.

The situation worked out best for all involved: Anantha got her way, Romeo had Anantha, and Mather had a place to call his own – which allowed Mather's aged and ill mother to take a room in a rest home, where she promptly died forever. And Romeo made no public lament over his new domestic development, a factor shocking in itself to his fellow regulars, one that Haycraft Keebler felt the need to applaud every night the three appeared together. *The triumph of the feminine, right before our eyes!* he exclaimed. *Not even our Romeo can withstand such compassionate power!*

The couple treated Mather to the movies once every weekend, an event tolerated but despised by Romeo because he detested kitsch and platitudes. He even took to driving his new charge to work at the Don Quixote – a ritual cherished by Mather Williams, who loved to ride anywhere, his large lean face plastered against the window, palms flat to the glass on either side of his head, staring out at the fleeting scenery and slow-moving pedestrians. He sang his songs as Romeo steered through the uneven streets. The only downside to these trips was that they invariably ended with Romeo fending off Mather's requests to allow him to drive.

— I'm a good driver, I tell you I know it! Drive the night away if you let me, drive it on home brother Romeo, drive it right on up to the green....

But these were modest sacrifices. Keeping an eye out on the damaged man, driving him to work at the same bar Romeo was headed to anyway – these acts allowed Romeo brief bursts of warm feeling that he was doing some good in the world, and such duties were small prices to pay for Anantha's contentment. Her satisfaction meant everything to him. For not only had he staked his feelings in her; he had identified Anantha as the portal to his most promising enterprise to date.

§

Later Romeo would maintain that despite his love for her, Anantha had introduced him to his downfall. *She destroyed me,* Díaz muttered to Beau, leaning in so that Chesley Sutherland could not overhear. And then in the next breath he admitted it was "just like a spic" to blame his failures on a particular woman, and that he strived to be above such things. Yet he blamed her.

Her job. That started it. At first Anantha stirred ideas of cheap profit and the celebration of sexual freedom, ideas Romeo cradled as close to his heart as a newly minted monk cradles his committed faith. Before Anantha, Romeo had no aggressive interest outside of money – which he had yet to make much of – and possibility, mulling over the how-to of influencing reality or fate or what-have-you to regard his life with more favor. He insisted that before Anantha he had held only a natural respect for sexual acts; he did his best under the yoke of a fatally repressed culture. Linking sex to money, however, transformed him. Anantha's conviction that a crusade could illuminate Americans to view sex as the summit of human beauty and achievement, rather than keeping the act shadowed beneath the shame of pornography, derailed him.

Amanda, as Anantha, was a popular stripper – or, as she phrased it, *erotic artist.* Intuitively he had placed her job within the spectrum of subversive activities he believed society needed in order to thrive. As he began to fall for her, he would sneak away from The Stone on nights she did not appear to recite her poetry, and steal to the door of the Primrose Flesh – never being so bold (or coarse) as to pay for a couch dance, no, not with the stinging lines of her verse still abuzz in his head. Instead he leaned into the thick red velvet curtains that draped one wall, inhaling the dust and cigarette smoke lodged there, the odor of stale alcohol, the very fibers humming with the turgid beat from the deejay's turntables, half-hidden in shadow but closely observed by the bouncer staff (Romeo invited suspicion naturally). He felt superior to the howling neckbones who slavered at the dancers on stage. Frat boys, relaxing pill-popped salesmen, dissipated lonely men absurdly falling in love – Romeo felt nothing but contempt for them all. The strut rhythms bombing the room, the flashing glow-pots and laser beams cutting the clouds of manufactured fog, the reckless legs akimbo shimmies of dancing girls – Romeo took it in and smiled, a man satisfied to know he stood firmly apart.

He was turned on himself. Not by the writhing bodies caught in the sweep of sheer light (though he admitted he wasn't immune to that and, new to the experience, found himself unable to turn away despite interior objections that he attended the club only for anthropological-slash-marketing research), so much as the amount of money being generated by subversion. That turned him on as much as the sight of Anantha on all fours, glistered in sweat, bare except for the g-string she kept clasped to her knees in order to abide by the city regulations that forbade full nudity.

So he pursued her until the affair was established; and then he convinced her to move in; and in turn she convinced him to give Mather Williams the cellar (*So I can look after the poor man,* she said, *and give your friends Beau and Glenda a break*). They would build their own family out of makeshift materials, she said.

Romeo agreed to everything she had to say. His thoughts were composed completely of Anantha (his Amanda): of her and her career, and most important, her future. Their future, together.

— You know what you should do, he asked, in his way, which always sounded more like a statement or directive than a normal question. Model. *You should model.* You could make good money.

— I do model. And I do make good money.

Romeo shook his head slowly, biting a smile through the sharp lines of his lips. They were lying in bed, a twin-sized mattress on the floor with no frame, encased in black sheets. He reached into a new leather box on the nightstand, and took out a camera.

— I'm talking about *real* modeling, he said. And making some *real* money.

Despite its popularity with the small group of patrons whom he despised, The Stone was speedily sinking into the mire of Romeo's intentions, the oblivion traditionally reserved for all businesses in Old Towne that did not cater to the alcoholic or sexually frustrated. He needed not just money, but what Haycraft's boy Lambret and his street-rat pals called *the big-face money*; the hard cash. He needed a new project to stimulate his passions.

At the time, all talk of economic promise turned on the booming possibilities of the Internet. Often Romeo would out-line to the other regulars his conceptual vision, whether they listened or not. His argument was that all new technologies quickly coalesced at society's lowest common denominator:

— Before Gutenberg you had your monks illuminating the gospels with dirty pictures and marginal limericks; with the printing press we got widespread erotica written by anonymous Victorians. When the camera came along, well let's just say I have a significant collection of not-artful nudes from the nine-teenth century. I thought only liberated women could be so depraved, but I own action photos from a century ago that prove me wrong.

In his view, the Web offered a streamlined pushcart for the hawking of dirty wares. He learned the technology and set up a site filled with photos of Anantha, Anantha with her girlfriends from the Primrose, Anantha's girlfriends with men of their own choosing. (Romeo considered it beneath him to perform in front of the camera. He believed his best talents resided in conceptual-ization, organization, and direction. He had the vision, after all.)

He got accounts with MasterCard, Visa, and American Express. Thus was born his third fiasco, for paying members only: The Philorgasmic Society. *Anyone could join.*

§

Success – the fact of it surprised even confident Romeo. The site sported a hip and funky design scanned from one of Mather's unruly paintings; Romeo traded banners with other fledgling Web sites, joined rings of free links, allowed gratuitous tours to generate just enough appetite for the real goods: penetration, girl-on-girl action, the money shots. At one point he reached just under three thousand members paying $3.95 a month (quickly jumping to $7.95, then leveling off two dollars lower), with Anantha's streaming-video image posing as virtual tour guide. Once Anantha ran out of new friends, Romeo placed ads in regional classifieds; then, in a fit of inspiration spurred by his desire to avoid actually paying the models, he encouraged members to send in their own amateur photographs. The swinging-community feel this fostered shot the site to its brief height, with members logging on as far away as Russia and the new Czech Republic. He pirated images from other galleries and posted them as his own. The site expanded to thousands of photographs ranging from art-house nudes to sex with animals and objects, and for a good stretch Romeo and Anantha were buying drinks for the entire house at the Don Quixote.

By his own admission, however, success had never been a rod Romeo could bear for long. Soon, a problem arose.

Anantha. Her image acted as the site's seductive host, leading members from room to room. Her voice narrated the naughty bedtime stories that she and Romeo would invent while lying about the Ruin, smoking hash, pushing one another to the most outrageous descriptions they could imagine as Mather Williams banged on pots and pans and sang his improvised songs in the basement.... Anantha was a hit; a star. She had that certain something. Nude pictures of Anantha in every variety of provocative pose abounded on the site, using every classic theme from the bored nurse to the adventurous farm girl. She frolicked with women, tilted with dildoes. But she was never allowed, pending the dictates of her Romeo, to be shown at work on a man. This absence became a cause of outrage within the ranks of membership.

E-mails started to arrive, sporadically at first and easy to ignore, but quickly escalating to the point that Romeo soon learned to dread opening the inbox. He turned the duty over to Anantha, who responded to as many letters as she could, in her best sympathetic tone. This led only to a doubling of traffic. At first she rolled her eyes at the adolescent perversion, the poorly punctuated paragraphs complaining *lissen I'm paying good money and enjoy your sight but okay I want to see Anantha blind-folded, with two men maybe three....* The details often caused her to giggle out loud; she shook her head at the shameless deviance expressed by men who thought themselves anonymous. She liked to relate the particulars to the boys at the bar, creating a strange scene in that she frankly described the performance these men wanted of her while simultaneously stroking the back of a quieted Mather Williams' head, the frail man's childlike body angled longingly toward her from his stool, mouth open and eyes closed, her slender, gentle hand starkly white against the dark curls of his remaining hair.

The number of e-mails mounted; the inventive designs for her body and its performance proliferated; the ideas were amusing, but they also sank deeply into Anantha. She was touched, really. She found marriage proposals, suicide pledges, invitations to dance at faraway strip clubs. Denunciations of her lover-the-webmaster. Each of them easily brushed away by a negligent smile at a pulsing computer screen, and yet ... she found herself thinking about these messages throughout her day; she found herself discussing them with her girlfriends, with Haycraft, with Lambret in the alley out behind the Don Q. Not one specific message affected her, but the surging waves of them created a kind of mood in her; an indefinable mood she came to label a *longing.* The growing number of men who wanted to see Anantha and were not too embarrassed to tell her so impressed her with a feeling of importance. And women, too; she had practically instigated an entire movement, a cause. Anantha began to wonder if she might actually have something to bring to the people. The site was beginning to bore her, anyway. Maybe she should do something to rock the boat a little bit? Without any intentions of her own she'd become a star of sorts, a new kind of star, one that had yet to be invented. Wasn't the whole idea to give the people what they wanted?

— Absolutely not, Romeo declared. You can share your body to view, but to violate it is my pleasure alone.

— Violate it? Anantha laughed. Ro-*may*-o (Anantha claimed him by pronouncing his name differently from everyone else, a habit that drew him to her), this isn't a big deal. It's just photos, baby. You and me together, it could be fun.

— I'm not even going to entertain the thought!

— But these e-mails we're getting, members are going to start dropping subscriptions if we don't get on this, doesn't that bother you?

— I am not listening!

— There are thousands of Web sites like ours, we can't afford to lose the members we have –

— I don't care, Romeo said. We share everything else with these suckers, I'm not going to add our lovemaking for their five bucks a month. Whatever happened to privacy, can't a man be intimate –

— No, we share everything about *me.* There's nothing of you out there, it's *me* they log on to see, not you. So I should make the decision. And I say we do it.

Romeo shook his head in the slow and deliberate manner that suggested he was testing the working mechanisms of his neck muscles. The flesh under his eyes sagged; his lips looked thinner than before, and whiter. He sharpened his nose between his thumb and forefinger, adamant in thought and point of view, exhaling loudly, puffed up with righteous certainty.

— No, it's not how we do things, he said with finality.

— We'll lose members! Anantha shouted. We're going to lose money!

— I don't care, Romeo answered.

He did begin to care, once the exodus began.

The members fled in droves. All because of her? he wondered. It didn't make sense. Sure, she was put together well enough – okay, she's beautiful, even; spectacularly so; *agreed* – but she was only one among many many girls. The louts could see whatever they wanted, just not with her. For a little while Romeo was able to comfort himself with contempt for the pathetic lives of these losers who whined and pined for two-dimensional images of his Anantha. *And I'm not even a talented photographer,* he admitted.

— Five dollars a month and they think they should get Venus cornholed by a bull, he complained to Beau.

How empty their worlds must be. How obsessive, these men. She was one face among the multitude. Furthermore, that face belonged to him. No; no. He refused. Romeo was the one calling the shots around here. Already he had practically taken on the hospice care of Mather Williams for her – what more could she want?

§

The money gave out to a trickle. The money ran low enough that he couldn't cover the burden of The Stone any longer, and he closed its double leaves with the consolation that he could make an excellent claim on his tax return. He declared that he

had lost interest in that endeavor long ago, once he learned
what subversion was really worth, through his Web site; at
The Stone there were just too many people relaxed and talking
nonchalantly about current events and whatever pathetic
creative projects they were dreaming of, everyone thought they
were an artist and this was pretty much the last thing Romeo
wanted to be associated with. The final straw for him came when
the discovery of bacterial life-forms on Mars stirred no interest
from his patrons; he could not understand why people didn't
latch onto the obvious fact that life is random and prompted by
chance, that all it requires is encouraging circumstance, not a
god. One night near the end he broke up a poetry reading by overtaking the microphone, confronting the people there from the
tiny stage with what he thought these discoveries suggested: *We
are in control, mankind is in the driver's seat, don't you see there is no
one to answer to when you die? Go home alone!* – and he was met
only with incredulous stares and the rustle of pages by poets
awaiting their turns. Romeo began to laugh at the crowd. He spat
on the floor, he threw down the mike with a thunderous boom.
Enough of this, he decided.

Romeo Díaz may have been the only man to close down his
business with a sense of satisfying triumph:

— Ha! I tell them, out on the streets with you, you fucking
patchoulis!

He beamed with greasy-smiled good cheer. He was no longer
buying drinks for anyone but himself; even Anantha was digging
in her purse to pay for her wine. A visible tension had grown
between them by the time he closed The Stone. She had been
fielding the members for months, and talking about it freely to
Beau and Glenda, to leering Chesley Sutherland, who gladly
encouraged her to follow her bliss. Haycraft tried to avoid the
subject; Lambret often turned the conversation to other topics.
Still the strain popped free before them all one night at the Don
Quixote.

The evening had already taken on the mood of a conflicted celebration: Due in large part to a highly fictionalized character deposition given by Beau, Sutherland had managed to beat his rap and get reinstated to the Montreux police force. Ostensibly everyone was happy for him – it did mean he would be around much less often. In private they each thought him very much an asshole, the worst-case scenario one envisions for a cop: beefy, impulsive, arrogant and ready to assert his authority, the type who comes in swinging the nightstick and leaves the questions for later. His saving grace was the weakness caused by asthma, his inhaler a sign of proof that he could go only so far. But nobody wanted to be on his bad side; he was legal with the gun again and his beat was Old Towne. This reality was worth each regular staking him a couple of beers as a way of congratulations, in hopes that maybe he would remember such good cheer should he ever confront them on a call one day.

Not to say that these were considerations for Anantha. She had no worries from Chesley. She was drinking her wine glass after glass and congratulating him on his post and applauding his good fortune in being allowed to pursue the life he felt it was his destiny to fulfill. *It's your bliss,* she said, *and you must follow it.*

— I don't have such luck myself, she proclaimed, loudly.

— I am not listening, Romeo said, in the same loud tone.

He made a point of looking straight across the bar at the stacked terraces of liquor bottles before the large mirror, at the carved-oak clock above, at the fishnet mannequin legs in spike heels (the DQ sported a curious shrine behind the bar: a gilt-edged portrait of J. Edgar Hoover flashing handcuffs, with two fishnet-clad mannequin legs demurely crossed below the frame), anywhere but at her. Anantha stood a couple of stools down from him, beside Chesley. By answering he had opened up the discussion to all gathered there. Her head pricked up at his voice – she was a good bottle and a halfpack of lipstick-ringed cigarette butts into the night by now – and she turned to him, setting down her long-stemmed glass on the half-wall after gently moving aside a stack of Haycraft's papers.

— You see, Chesley, I'm being kept from my career by the one person who should be a thousand percent behind me, she said, after a dreamy, regretful pause, staring at Romeo.

He refused to look at her.

— That must be awful, Chesley sympathized.

— You have got to be kidding, Romeo said.

— I'm a star, she called back. A new kind of star.

Mather passed between them to return a push broom to the closet behind the bar; the word caught in his ear and he started mumbling into one of his free-associative riffs, his tongue ticker-taping the random thoughts from his head, voice rising above the noise he made opening the closet door, knocking buckets aside as he replaced the broom: *star, star, there's a heaven and a star for you Miss Amanda, a star is born in the sky every day ... the stars come out at night, star light star bright ... my momma say ever star you see been dead since before you were born....* He held the small door open with one craggy knotted hand; his voice stopped and he stared inside. The parade of words ceased as quickly as they had started.

Romeo looked about with put-upon incredulity, wide-eyed as though to say, *Do you people see what I have to deal with?* He assured Mather that everything was all right and told him not to get upset. He then turned on his stool so that his back was now to the black man – who remained gazing deeply into the closet, having completely forgotten that Romeo (that anyone) was there behind him. Romeo grabbed the moment to speak some as-he-saw-it sense to Anantha. He reminded her that their Web site was just a hobby that had turned out gloriously lucrative. For a while. He pointed out that a career could not be made on such hobbies, that life and careers were all flux and change, and that perhaps she should think of something more lasting, as her beauty, significant though it was, would not endure forever, or even for very long. A sad reality he would have to suffer alongside her, true, but one that he was willing to suffer. He asked about her political science degree, and what about that? He had not missed the fact that she had failed to sign up for any courses that semester – what about that, huh? Why?

The regulars turned in her direction with the uniform focus of an audience at a tennis match following the serve. Anantha inclined her chin and bit her upper lip – to firm her resolve? To prevent saying something extreme beforc the rest? The gesture and the length of time she indulged in it seemed significant to those watching. It wasn't until she stopped and thrust her chin forward that she made her case:

— Yes, once I really wanted that degree, I admit that. But now it seems a false path. It's useless to me, even the idea of it, something I started out of innocent ambition. You know, it's like I thought the degree would legitimize me somehow. But what I really liked was the dancing. And then when all that money started pouring in, it occurred to me: Who am I trying to impress here? I never talk to my parents, you know that. I'm not ashamed of what I do. In fact it's a gift I give to the world. And what kind of life could I have as a professor, catfighting year round and writing for obscure journals nobody reads, hoping to get tenure? I want to have an effect on this world. Considering the number of members we've had and comparing them with the number of readers of poli-sci journals, there's no question who people are paying more attention to. I mean regular people, you and me and everybody else in this bar. Name me one political scientist that has ever made a difference, she said.

— Why, Plato! Haycraft interjected, physically incapable of resisting such discussions.

He spilled his pint of beer with the energy of the gesture.

— There's an entire list, he continued. Machiavelli, Hobbes, Locke, Rousseau….

The others shushed him immediately. Anantha tried to ignore him, her face reflecting a degree of tried patience, eyes remaining on her true challenger, Romeo. She repeated herself, this time adding a slight variation:

— Name me one political scientist, *of our day and age*, who has made the slightest difference.

Neither Romeo nor Haycraft (who prided himself on knowing his classics, not contemporaries) had an answer for her.

— Uh huh. And on top of that, Anantha continued, after a long wait through the loud TV commercials and no one willing to challenge her, with the nature of what I do for a living and how it's hardly a kept secret, what self-respecting university is going to hire me?

— Are you kidding? Romeo asked. Universities would kill to have someone with your profile on faculty. Political science as a major would jump two hundred percent!

Anantha shrugged him off. She did not care, she said. She pointed out that an unfortunate and lamentable aspect of his character was that he easily fell prey to his own wishful thinking. Not that this was without its charms. But over the past several months maybe she had learned something important about herself, and what about that? She wanted money; preferably lots of it. Regard. A comfortable lifestyle, rimmed with a touch of celebrity, preferably of a scandalous nature as that seemed the kind most often remembered and most suitable to her personality. Someday she could parlay her reputation into a big tell-all memoir, or maybe even get her own talk show.

— You know, *once my beauty has gone away*, she let drop with fatal sarcasm, eyes to the lattice ceiling.

Beau pushed another glass of wine to her over the bar. *Fuckin' A right*, he said, grinning. *Don't take any guff from your old man, Anantha. That's how Glenda goes about it.* The comment set the listeners to chuckling, a perfect example of Beau's gift to simultaneously diffuse and encourage a situation for his patrons' enjoyment. But Haycraft did not laugh. He was observing closely, digging a little deeper than the rest. He pulled off his glasses and looked at Anantha intently, then Romeo, before wiping his eyes with one hand and returning the glasses to his face. Romeo was preparing an answer.

— Okay, he began. Let's pretend I can ignore my scruples and entertain this seriously for a moment. Let's follow your logic. Name me one scandalous piece of ass that has, quote, made a difference, end quote, that you suddenly feel so strongly about.

— There's an entire list, she echoed Haycraft. Helen of Troy, Sappho, Mata Hari, Marlene Dietrich and Marilyn Monroe … Jane Fonda, even.

Jane Fonda! Romeo and Haycraft roared at once. Lambret began to tug at Hay's sleeve in order to distance him from what Lambret considered an essentially private argument. Even as Haycraft stepped back, however, he managed to interject:

— But Fonda is despised; nobody with any taste, discernment, intelligence takes that woman seriously!

— She has *made a difference,* Anantha insisted, softly. I'm not on a crusade here to change the world. It's enough to do what you do well, make your presence and thoughts known, tweak people's heads. I celebrate sexuality and people need to hear that.

Fuckin' A right, groused Chesley Sutherland, mimicking Beau. This time nobody laughed.

— Listen, your thoughts are not what these guys are asking from you, Romeo said. They'd be disappointed to learn you have any, in fact.

Only now did he appear to fully realize the attention of the others lined parallel to the both of them, blocked only by the half-wall. The entire tribe was there, even those who have yet to be referred to, as they were the silent drinkers whose lives were impossible to penetrate: Johnny Reb, the pawn shop owner who was also licensed to preside over marriages and whose real name was never known; Wink McCormack, the long-haired university professor who referred to himself as "the alcoholic adjunct";

Tyrone Jeffers, the yellow-skinned black man who said he started drinking because his own family gave him a hard time for having such a light shade, and who used his cane to draw napkins and the peanut bowl down the bar to his place, and who liked to play practical jokes with his dentures. They were all watching and listening and keeping to themselves as best they could alongside Beau, Glenda, Mather, Chesley, Lambret, and Haycraft. Even happenstance diners had found their attention involuntarily drawn to the discussion at the bar. Romeo's lips bunched in scorn; his left ear seemed to bother him and he scratched at it incessantly. He shrugged with emphatic finality, and turned on his stool so that again he faced the bar, only Beau and Mather now within his range of vision, the rest just reflections in a foggy mirror he tried to ignore. In the long pause that followed, he raised one finger to Beau and murmured his desire for a glass of red wine, now, as apparently it led one to rosy speculations of the future.

Anantha had much more to say. Now that her reservations and needling doubts had been raised about the direction of their business interests, she thought it a fine time to address a few other concerns, such as their Ruin and her fatigue – that was the precise word she wanted, *fatigue* – of living there. They lived in a squalor inappropriate to the glamour necessitated by their Web site project, she said, and she was sick of these bohemian attempts at domesticity in a dilapidated Ruin (*ruin* slipping out with all the derision her soft, reedy voice could muster). She launched into a list of complaints: holes still gapped the ceiling and kitchen floor; the floorboards needed to be sanded, buffed, and sealed, since those warped cracks between them clung with dust so thick that no amount of mopping could erase it despite her and Mather's best efforts. Many walls were still begging for a face-lift of joint compound before she could even consider repainting them. She was sick of washing with a handheld showerhead in a rust-rotted tub with only a white plastic curtain for privacy; she was sick of having to wear plastic sandals into her own bathroom in order to avoid the thick fungal scum thriving among the tiles. They needed to insulate the basement to keep Mather from living amid stone walls, too, which she thought was a cruel and medieval fate and the likely cause of his new cough.

The essence of what she was saying was that soon she would be leaving. Romeo was worldly enough to understand this, and he did not know what to do. He understood why; just as he understood that, in his own arrogant and cold way, he loved her – loved her voice humming to herself when she fried up a favorite egg-and-cheese sandwich for Mather, and how otherwise on those rare occasions when she cooked they did not eat dinners so much as disasters; loved her need to keep the ruined rooms spotlessly clean (save the bathroom, which kind of frightened them both), brightly lit with frosted lights, the walls painted a hard alabaster eggshell (well, the rotting plaster was alabaster-*ish*); he loved how she had gone so far as to buy large slates of drywall herself, in a hopeful bid that their presence would guilt him into working on home improvement, but which so far remained in disconsolate rows along the main hallway. (Romeo had renovated only the old parlor into the main studio for his photography.) Otherwise she preferred the rooms bare, with a minimum of decor – a hanging plant here, an unadorned vase there. She was the only person he knew who could hold a sponge in one hand as she launched into an argument for a First Cause or Cosmic Designer (she believed in a presence or consciousness that was unknowable and therefore God – Romeo had never been able to break her tenacity on this point). He loved her passion for living things (plants) and her ineptitude at tending them – the Ruin comprised a floral graveyard. Her compassion for the brainsick Mather, and how in witness of that he had discovered a slight awakening of his own capacity for charity.... Romeo would miss all of this and more if she were to leave. Therefore, he must love her.

Yet he was thin of trust. He felt incapable of showing any candid emotion save anger. He was a strange man and knew it; a restless and reckless man who disliked any manifestation of weakness whatsoever – and yet he made his pursuits with only half a heart, his quests forever capricious and rambling, now swerving wide of the goal, now abandoning it midway, as one orders a fresh drink having forgotten the glass still half-full and within arm's reach. And so after this night of argument before his unwanted audience at the Don Q, Romeo watched silently as Anantha, his Amanda, slowly began to withdraw and leave, one tick off her heart at a time, until at last she left him standing helplessly, static in expression.

§

What triggered her actual departure was the instance of Romeo's grandest humiliation. He passed the better part of an afternoon in dreariness, scotch, and headache, crimped by Mather's blather over Anantha's beauty, his need for new colored markers, and how much he wished Romeo would allow him – just once – the chance to drive his old BMW. *Put me in the driver's seat, just like the mankind you say!* he implored. Romeo did his best to ignore such beseechings; he promised Mather (as he had already so many times before) to take him to Frederick Park one Saturday after-noon, when there was time once he got his business running well again and smoothed things over with Anantha, and give him a lesson in controlling the wheel of a car. Between bursts of assur-ances to Mather, Romeo mocked Haycraft's grandstandings that to heal the world one must reconcile with feminine principles.

— Tenderness, compassion, the generously mothering hand leading with charity and mercy....

— Ah, my ass, Hay. *My ass*, insisted Romeo.

He folded up the file he had been scanning without interest, applications with bios and photos of girls answering his regional classifieds to perform for the Philorgasmic Society. He was tired of looking at these girls. He was tired, period, and decided to go home early. Certainly that was the cause of his failure – a general burning-out – and not anything else (not a failing inherent in him). Came home to discover Anantha had decided to save their ailing Web site by giving the people what they wanted.

The Ruin's clean parlor greeted Romeo with bright umbrella lights shining off the alabaster walls; the dark leather couch had been covered with a single pale blue sheet. Tempest handled the camera. She was a friend of Anantha's from the Primrose, once a hurricane of promised hard-thighed sex now sunk to a bloated sack of Oxycontin obsession. Anantha was readying her makeup, wearing red currant negligee, nude stockings, a black garter, the whole show. A boy – *Haycraft's boy* – anxious in baggy dungarees and a dirty white tank-top undershirt, withstood Tempest's attentions as she unbuttoned his pants to apply a foundation brush to his lower abdomen. (A bit of overkill for a simple Webcast film, in Romeo's view.) The boy's bulky Doc Martens stood soiled with mud, unlaced. In either hand he held a hammer and screwdriver, and a bucket of paint was open at the foot of a ladder near the sheeted couch. The bored housewife seduces the helpful young neighbor kid. Without Romeo they couldn't invent a scenario more original than a pictorial out of *Penthouse* circa 1977.

Honey! exclaimed Anantha, her fingers interlaced before her, nervous expectation alive among them. Her painted nails fluttered with the same red currant as her nightdress.

— I thought you'd close down the Q tonight, she said.

Romeo did not answer. Instead, he studied her. He studied her for what passed as long moments, anxious nerve-withering moments, his face masked in slack, bland indifference. Finally he winced, scratched at the bridge of his nose.

— Bitch, he mustered, in a tone of near-surprise and absolute distaste.

The word startled her and animated him. He loosened his tie with a fierce clutch and rip at his own throat. Anantha did not move; she could only watch him, having not yet rebounded from the surprise of his arrival. She felt awkwardly denuded in the bright light, caught dressed perfectly for one occasion but finding herself in quite another one, like the common anxiety dream of standing naked before schoolmates. Romeo made toward her with a determined violence everywhere apparent in his body; he seemed ready to strike her; he even had his right hand raised – but then he stopped. Suddenly he appeared thoughtful, and only rubbed the back of his head with his palm. He turned and took a few deliberate steps toward Lambret.

Tempest shuffled out of his way. The boy straightened himself against the wall, his eyes declining to meet the older, angry man's, where quiet fury danced. It made Romeo smile – not so much an actual smile as a baring of teeth – and inch closer, emboldened by the dramatic difference in their heights. With sharp satisfaction he heard the clumsy clang at Lambret's feet as the tools slipped to the floor. His chin nearly caught the boy between the eyes. His lips pulled back again to allow breath stale from cigarettes and whisky to wash through his long yellow teeth and over the young, simple face.

— Him? Romeo asked.

His voice rasped. He sniffed at Lambret, and allowed another long, infuriating pause to sift the air, bestowing a sense of impending awfulness. When he moved suddenly, spinning back to face Anantha, everyone else flinched, and again this brought the cruel grasp of a smile (a teeth-baring slash across his face that Romeo had an innate gift for) as he repeated the question – *him?* Nobody answered. They returned only open-mouthed stares, leaving the query to waft in the still air sharp with the dust burning off the camera lights. He turned again to the boy, whose pale face reddened visibly in the stark light, despite the pancake makeup. Lambret stuttered as he tried to speak an apology, some excuse, still refusing to meet the cutting eyes; he stuttered as he tried to say that he did not want any trouble.

Laughter, then: Romeo gave a high-pitched whinny of a laugh. So much about the kid already upset him. That lithe, thin body of a teenage girl that promised to blossom late; those delicate, breakable features. His fine cheekbones and large, heavy-lidded eyes – and did he curl those long black lashes?; his thick locks of spiral curls that hid the ears and draped the jaw before spilling onto his feeble shoulders; his bird-boned chest and arms, not exactly scrawny but pliable, small, softly contoured. Every physical aspect of the boy upset him. Disturbed him. Romeo hated the appearance of innocence, especially in what he knew to be soiled.

— You want the boy? Romeo asked. The boy likes other boys.

— I want the shots, Anantha answered evenly.

— The shots, repeated Romeo.

He wished aloud he had thought to bring home a bottle of Beau's cheap watered scotch, or at least a good jug of wine. Something to smash and spread a stain all over the floor or one of these perfect-white walls. He wondered aloud what Hay thought of all this, and did he know Lambret was here, expanding his business opportunities? Again, no one answered him. He felt like a high-school teacher confronted by an unprepared class, throwing out his questions to dumb silence. As a kid in those situations he knew a quiz was coming soon. He reacted now in the same way as that imaginary teacher, glaring at Tempest (whom he detested for her addiction) and smiling as she shrank behind the camera, pathetically, as though she thought she might hide behind the tripod (*his* camera! *his* tripod!). Now, easing his tie from his neck entirely and casting it aside, he announced:

— I'll give you shots, dammit. Start that camera going.

— Ro-*may*-o..., Anantha began.

He lunged for her, grabbing her wrists and yanking her to him.

He pressed his palm to the small of her back and pushed her so that their groins pressed together in a weird, tangolike coupling, a dance she hesitated to join but allowed herself to be carried by. Biting at her neck, his fingers straining white – pink at the bulging knuckles – Romeo bellowed at her to relax. *I'm not going to hurt you, dear.* And in the fast moments following the others could see Anantha begin to loosen, to accept him, easing from embarrassed misgivings. He stopped only when he realized he had yet to hear any action from the camera.

— Let's get on top of it, Tempest! Don't tell me you've dosed already, we don't want to disappoint the public! Let us capture the moment!

Tempest fiddled with the tripod, sighing. She peered through the lens then raised her head again, unsure. Her weight shifted from one thick hip to the other, pushing tight in a miniskirt she once had the right to wear. She stared at the two of them clutching one another.

— Romeo, you want I direct you all?

— We'll manage, thanks, we've been here before. Just follow and shoot.

He seized the interruption to shrug off his raincoat, his sport jacket.

The camera started in clicks and whirs.

At this point the room narrowed to a nervous clearing of a throat as Lambret found his voice. He asked if he should just go on home. Should he do anything with these tools? Again Romeo stopped, his frustration now reflecting impatience with all these delays rather than the original anger at what he would later come to think of, to publicly announce as – once sobered and calm and his humiliation complete – his betrayal. He kept Anantha's arms clamped to her sides; they remained as if caught in some twisted dance, her eyes still wide and uncertain to his face. He did not look away from her; instead he smiled, a true smile now, and from over one shoulder cooed,

— Home? Home to where, your daddy? No, I want you to stay. Why not pick up the video camera, little lamb?

I want you to see this, Romeo said. *You may learn something.*

Two statements that would later compound his embarrassment. Romeo was incapable of forgetting anything, and what a curse that was. His pride, the cock confidence in being a healthy man – how hollow it turned out to be. How inescapable.

Romeo tore at the negligee in his best stab at appearing rapacious. He wanted to devour her, wanted this want made absolutely clear to the camera. But the camera was *it*; the camera posed the problem. Never before had he found himself so conscious of performance, so – literally and figuratively – naked and exposed. As he grasped Anantha's breasts and hips, gnawed at the supple meat inside her thigh, ripped away her stockings – usually big turn-ons for him – he could not avoid the presence of that eye in the lens tracking every movement and gesture, every blemish on his skin, every odd hair out of place, every sad fold of flab. Odd considerations came to mind: Was he doing it right? How did he look to someone who had never seen him before? To someone who did not know his charm? Was the scene hot enough? His body – he would not expect a poll of women to gush over the possibilities, but he was fit enough. Wasn't he? His cock would frighten no one but it would do. Or would it? Did Anantha think so? Would everyone else? He suffered a brief but incandescent vision of a thousand men sitting alone before their computers, bathed in blue monitor light, full-sizing thumbnail images of Romeo naked with Anantha and … *and laughing*. That bruising laughter that began as a loose mouth topped by thin, simian upper lip that stretched slowly wide into a tight line; a grin, a giggle, and soon the mocking bursts of full-scale hilarity.

Romeo's caresses turned stiff, awkward. He grumbled that they should at least provide some music, some whiplash salsa or something for chrissakes. Anantha sensed the problem; she could smell agitation in his sweat; she tasted it on his neck. She tried to encourage him with her sighs and her own attentions, but after a while even she began to feel self-conscious and inexpert. And the force of her sighs and the exertion evident in them only heightened Romeo's awareness that this was not pleasure or thrill, but *work*. A job. First he sensed, then sought her helpfulness, even as it shamed him that she recognized the need to do so. Anantha did all she could; no blame could be slung at her for lack of effort. Her jaw tired, her tongue ached. To no profit. A dead fish cannot be resuscitated.

It seemed they labored for hours and reached only the most limited level of success. Romeo's thoughts drifted from his desire to "devour" her to wondering what one could mean by "devour" in terms of a sexual act, leading him to distracting mental pictures of certain insect behavior that did not help at all. Then came the more immediate concern of performer and audience; then the panicked realization of how much time and film had elapsed without worthwhile visuals from him. Soon he was wondering at the patience of the others in the parlor.

Finally, he stood.

Romeo moved away from Anantha with a sigh, stepping to his clothes, acutely aware that Tempest had stopped taking pictures long ago. Lambret had begun testing video shots of the windows, the floor, the tight clasp of Tempest's skirt, his own hands. Even at his young age he understood the tactlessness of recording a man's humiliation of himself. (Romeo would never forgive him that tacit understanding.) In an agonizing silence broken only by his faked yawn, Romeo slid his legs into the silk paisley boxers, the worsted trousers; he slipped on his socks while standing. Anantha remained on the sofa and watched him. She reached for cigarettes, lit one, allowed him to finish dressing, said,

— Baby, it happens.

Romeo's gruff laugh sent a stripe of accidental spit to the hardwood floor, his hand jumping to his jaw too late to stop it. He

wanted to say *of course it does*. He wanted to tell them all he had
drunk quite a bit this day already. They should know that Mather
seemed dispirited all afternoon and Romeo did not know why
and it gnawed at him.... Instead, shame turned his face from
the usual mix of olive-umber to the purple of slapped skin. He
patted down his hair and felt the flopsweat dampness. It was
then that he realized the wet everywhere upon him, salting his
lips, stinging his eyes, saturating his clothes. Silence, more
unwieldy and resilient silence, careered around the room.

He had to recover somehow. He needed to save some modicum
of face, control, pride. It was time to drop orders.

— Well. (He placed his hands in his pockets, took them out
again.) Well now, we still need to get those shots, don't we. Hop
in there, boy.

Anantha sat up.

— No honey, I'm too tired now, let's do it another time –

— Do it! This is what you wanted, now you do it!

He grabbed the camera off the tripod and pushed Tempest
aside, checking its focus and speed and growling – with just a
foretaste of hopeful satisfaction – that it was a good thing the
scene didn't work out since the photos would have been useless
in any case. He barked at Lambret to put down the video camera
and get to work even as he yanked it from him, hurling the boy
toward the sofa in the middle of the room where Anantha
remained nude but in doubt.

— Come on kid, we haven't got all night, you want to get paid
for your troubles, don't you? For all that missed homework? Let's
go, pants off! Let's see what the little stud's got packing there,
jump in the saddle, pal, she can be a wild ride, I promise you!
Rolling....

A touch of smugness slipped over his embarrassment; surely
some of the sting would skulk away if he spread around the
humiliation. Romeo was certain the boy's nervousness would
keep the evening from profit.

But this was only a hopeful delusion. Anantha was gentle with Lambret, patient, fond, and engaging. In no time they had the shots she wanted.

§

The ensuing weeks comprised a personal apocalypse for Romeo. Nights came when he drifted from the bar with drink in hand and scattered the hours over a series of scotches in uncharacteristic, languishing silence, the darkening room gathering over his face in a drawn-down inward scowl, the man wrapped deep into an impenetrable solitude. He stumbled to the Steinway in the Theatre Room to finger awkward and insouciant scales, not songs. He wanted to be alone, he wanted everyone to know he wanted to be alone. And then the boy was there, too, and he had to suffer witness to that, Lambret striding in with a laugh next to Haycraft Keebler (*that big fake!* Romeo beefed to Beau), often holding the older man's hand. The mere sight of the kid filled him with masochistic, disgusting pleasure. The girlish boy steeped Romeo in a cool self-loathing he came to cherish, a loathing he accelerated with more alcohol, happy to find he was still capable of feeling anything at all.

And couldn't it have all turned out otherwise? Why couldn't capital-C chance have thrown him just a cookie crumb of favor there? The failed night of shooting – it could have convinced Anantha that Romeo had been just in his decree against her working with men, that it wasn't about his own twisted morals or pathetic jealousies. In fact, had it not been for the late hour and all the cigarettes and whisky, he could have spun the meaning of that night more his way. He should have sent the boy out when he had asked. Instead he got to watch him have his woman, got to see the strange smile Anantha gave Lambret afterward, the gentle trace of her fingers over his neck, a hazy and soothing look Romeo realized he had never seen from her himself, directed at the little bastard.

— One indisputable law I've always held is that some people are simply born losers, he confessed to Beau. It never occurred to me that I might be one of them. Never even occurred to me.

— Don't be so hard on yourself. You got to pick your moments.

— Sometimes the moments pick you, Romeo answered.

"The weeks of nightmare," he called them, once they were over. Weeks when his conceits abandoned him and he was left staggering behind a bustling Anantha in vain hopes of some absolution. Some pardon or vindication that Anantha did not aim to grant him, having no clue to what there was to absolve him of. She did not think any less of him for the failure. (*I've known him long enough to understand every part of him works,* she told Lambret. *Not everyone feels right in front of a camera. All sorts of shit happens.*) As far as she was concerned the entire event was a business transaction she now needed to capitalize upon. The only lesson to take from it was that Romeo was best suited behind the camera and not before it. What irritated her, what drew her down the descending arc of disappointment in him and their life together, was how such an "inconsequential lapse" had transformed her man. His masculinity, his casual indifference, his guile – these were the qualities that had attracted Anantha, and in an instant they disappeared, leaving her with a stranger, a beleaguered Romeo scurrying behind her, craving her approval.

When she announced her plan to make a national tour of strip clubs to advance her swipe at fame, Romeo disappointed her with his speed of agreement. *You should have been on the road long ago,* he said. *We would have had adventure and been rich at once.*

He scheduled her performance dates himself, making the phone calls and negotiating with appalling men, the kind who coughed directly into the phone and asked what drugs they should have available for her and dickered over percentages to a mystifying degree. Romeo planned the calendar, he designed posters and advertising, he filed faxed contracts and booked hotel reservations. He set her up with a credit card holding a large cash limit for unforseen expenses. All of it very useful and welcome help, Anantha admitted. But the atmosphere it furnished – how he went about such duties – diminished her respect for him: He showed none of his usual initiative or authority; he took her orders and fulfilled her wishes. He gave no hint that he was acting in her interests as her manager planning to come along on the road (in fact Romeo assumed it a foregone conclusion that he wasn't welcome, and had arranged for a professional to take on that task). They lost the sense of being collaborators in a scheme, co-conspirators exploiting Anantha's skills to rake in the cash and laugh at the squares together. What he had become was her sympathetic secretary. A toady tuckler, Beau would call it; her bootlicking publicist. He appeared to revel in the disdain she was no longer trying to hide.

Anantha hit the road in the spring of that year, and everyone recognized that she was not just traveling; she was *gone*. Romeo withered; his daily activities shrank to caretaking Mather Williams, sitting cross-legged beside him for long hours beneath a haze-birthing sun, on a concrete sidewalk bench, watching the scrawny black hands scrawl out the savage art. He paid him a dollar per song just to see the smile of crooked teeth crease Mather's simple face. When he eventually ventured out from beneath his wounded cocoon – before anger and outrage filled him with purpose again – the regulars were allowed to enter into discussion with him on two sole subjects: Mather's creativity (Romeo planned a recording session for the a cappella songs, once he came up with the funds), and detailed updates on the growing phenomenon of Anantha's American Tour. Details that were wholly invented by his yearning imagination, since he had not heard word one from the woman whom, he liked to brag, he had made into a star.

He gave himself a touch of credibility by now referring to her as simply Amanda, her real name.

Eventually, over a graded stage of days, he began to appear again with a more focused air, with an almost determined cast to his manner; now he carried a manila envelope under his arm everywhere, and set it unopened beside him on the bar, protecting it with one outstretched palm should anyone decide to sit next to him. Some regulars assumed it was a file for Mather's work; others said it was for pictures of Anantha on tour he had yet to scan for the Society's Web site, or else further applicants. They avoided asking him about it, as they thought his newfound purpose in facilitating the goals of others – Anantha, Mather (although he still refused to let the man drive the '68 Beemer) – embarrassed him.

He might have agreed, had he been asked. He did not know he had such depths of feeling within himself. This recognition led to a sense of bitterness, an aura of indignities suffered, a resentment that came with confronting the facts of his humanity. His contempt for others bottomed out as he found himself on equal ground, and that ground felt unfamiliar.... The limp failure before the camera, the abandonment by the woman he had grown to love, the fact that his caretaking of Glenda's Child of God gave him a responsibility he was learning to enjoy (he actually *looked forward* to time spent with Mather) – these personal scandals were erased by the realization that he had transformed into the ultimate anathema he could imagine: Romeo Díaz was officially a bore.

THE
NIGHTS
AT
THE
DON
QUIXOTE

BEAU STILES STOOD ON THE SIDE-walk, his back pronged by the steel curve of a parking meter, and stared implacably into the gaping hole that used to be his plate-glass window. Three large storefront windows lined the street side of the Don Q in a stuttered, horizontal row, lending patrons a view of the neighborhood surrounds while inviting anyone outside to the warmth within. He read the windows now, left to right, in the increase of summer heat: the first now bereft of anything but a shark's mouth of angry glass teeth; the second a cratered moonscape left from the impact of the steel-mesh wastebasket (spray-painted gold) that now lay against the curb. Oddly, the third window appeared untouched. He had seen worse damage before, and counted himself lucky. The yeggs had raided much of the liquor stock but otherwise the building had escaped any more lasting damage.

He knew how this all went down – the bodies running with the heat and that strange mix of panic and elation, spying the gold-shining wastebaskets at once as they realized the windows, the windows of a place owned by whites. He tried not to take this personally. At the same time, he tried to memorize as many faces as he could remember from the streets that morning, when the promise of the day turned bad and the crowd went all hincty: The laughs turned to leers, the smiles to scowls, and then ... the cops show and everyone's hitting the bricks. As if no one expected cops to show and freaked at the sight.

Beau had seen it all before.

He knew riots. He knew protest and how to go about it, having marched with Glenda and his younger brother all through the early sixties in Alabama, in Atlanta, in Montreux. As a white he had never gone to jail for it, and that disappointed him. It was like lacking a necessary credential. Though he'd never pushed any situation in order to make a point. Unlike his brother Madison – who had disappointed him, too, and who went much too far (in Beau's eyes) in pursuit of the most extreme credentials, disappearing underground for twelve years after planting a bomb at a Federal Bank in Richmond, Virginia, in 1974. Beau was just paranoid enough to believe that the loans he and Glenda needed to secure in order to open their club were not going to go through (they had been dismissed before) until Madison turned up under some assumed name somewhere. Which turned out to be Montana. Which came as no surprise to Beau, since he was the one who had phoned in the tip that unleashed the feds – so maybe karma said he deserved the broken windows in the end. His brother wouldn't be eligible for parole for another six years. That fact fettered Beau Stiles with a harsh degree of guilt even though he did believe he had done the right thing, having long disagreed with Madison's extremity – *deeply*, in fundamental terms of basic personal philosophy. He had consoled himself by rationalizing that now they could argue these points face-to-face, albeit via telephones to accommodate the soundproof plexiglas that divided them.

At least hypothetically. Madison refused to see his brother or even Glenda on their happenstance visits. Twelve years into a federal sentence and Beau's brother still managed to avoid him.

Fundamentally – as a question of intrinsic characteristics – Beau did not believe in extreme behavior: Protests could work, yes, they could potentially change social ills, but they had to be gone about peacefully, firm, in phalanxes of nonviolence – the Gandhi method. To acquire real change you had to be smarter and more stubborn and more calm than your opposition. To martyr them only made them that much more steadfast in their stance and demonized your cause; to squall in rage and stomp your boots only made you appear insane, easily dismissed from the debate.

Beau had his own battles, besides.

Returning one heavy wastebasket to its proper street corner, he would have liked to remind his brother of that point. He would have liked to have reminded, now, whoever it was who had destroyed the windows of his club. He would have liked to say to them: *I'm solid, man, I want the same as you do, lamp your eyes elsewhere*. But he had abandoned trying to convert anyone else to his own points of view a long time ago. He could not handle other people's hysteria. If you want to help the world, he remembered to himself, you cannot condemn it. Wasn't that a line from church? Or somewhere else? *Our misery is the result of our weakness*. He could not pinpoint the aphorism exactly, but knew it wasn't his. He was not wise enough to have coined it.

Still, the broken windows galled him: He and Glenda had elected to skip the morning shift and head instead to the word-of-mouth march in protest of the city's latest casualty, Maxwell Hayden. They had hoped some good could be made of an awful situation. So it was hard not to take the damage personally. He had been out there *on their side*, after all – this was the thanks he got? For coming off solid with the neighbors?

Beau gazed over the splash of glass littering the floor of his restaurant and crunched kernels of it under his sturdy boots, and sighed. It bugged him that he felt no surprise.

§

He was a boy, he was black, he had this thing for crystal meth. Chesley Sutherland insisted that what the public never knew about Maxwell Hayden was that he had a sealed juvenile record long as the forgotten railway lines, and that the offenses were mostly violent. *Okay maybe he didn't go out in the most fair fashion*, went the Sutherland View (spat in contempt, in grimace, as though it tasted bad to speak such things), *but this world is no worse for the loss*. Beau argued that the kid was only sixteen, joy-riding a hot SUV when two cops shot him to death.

— He's got his hands on the wheel at ten and two o'clock, man, debated Beau. The department's not even challenging that, and it's not right, Sutherland, and you know it, and people need to see and hear that other people know it, too.

Haycraft Keebler echoed the sentiment. Hayden was the third offender to die at the hands of the police in ten months' time, each under unclear circumstances. The police department did little to clarify these situations, and this time around the mob response was quick and explicit. A slow, stifling summer broke majestically on the streets of Old Towne: Beau was out there with his convenience-store coffee while Glenda walked through the crowd, saying her hellos to familiar faces. Beau listened to the fiery slogans chanted by the chorus of massed voices, gazed at the faces of the sneering churls, and allowed himself a comfortable sense of nostalgia, smiling at the signs of protest that bobbled among fists raised to the sky. Then mounted police arrived and the crowd surged, and he was in frantic search of his wife.

He didn't see her immediately and so scuttled to the outskirts of the crowd, keeping off to one side and rushing ahead through front yards. Soon he was vaulting iron fences to keep pace as the horde gained momentum, doing his best with his old body, lungs huffing. Then the formless mass morphed tentacles of groups and gangs that slipped down into the side streets and alleys, and he did not know which way to go. He tried to stick with the main stem that stayed on the major avenue, watching as two young men left the pavement to walk over hot engine hoods, kicking playfully at the drivers who dared honk their horns. Girls danced on the sidewalk, cackling at the catcalls, their hips ashimmy and hands clapping. In a way the scene felt almost like an irrepressible party that was threatening only to get out of hand. But Beau could recognize a powder keg when he smelled one: the stench of sweat and exhaust heavy in his nostrils, and the noise – car horns and idling engines and horses clacking their hooves, police commands growing in urgency and responses from the demonstrators turning angrier, radio static and laughter, heavy bass beats thumping from boom boxes. He could not find his wife; every face seemed a stranger, and angry. When the police cruisers arrived and cut off the entrance to Frederick Park, the rocks began to fly.

It is difficult to imagine a riot in winter. In winter a death like Maxwell Hayden's in a stolen SUV means outraged letters to the editor and braying at Aldermen meetings and a promise by the police chief to appoint investigators; in summer it means a frantic Beau Stiles bolts from beneath the trees to stir up Mather Williams aghast on the street corner, clutching his case of art tools, and pulling the man to the safety of a back alley. It means hoping your wife is still as tough a girl as she was in the old days, and can take care of herself. It means stopping short in shock at the sight of Haycraft Keebler railing through a bullhorn on concrete steps, smacking his hand on a golden wastebasket. In summer a riot means arrests, stopped traffic, thrown bottles, sidewalk trash baskets pushed through storefront windows. A free-for-all.

That night all of Old Towne felt mildly electric at the edges. The regulars were the only ones in the place. The band that was supposed to play had canceled out of safety concerns and Beau didn't fault them for it, though he did worry about the precedent it set. So the Don Q rooms were quiet – they didn't turn on the jukebox, and kept the lights low. The television murmured coverage of arrests and outrage; Romeo passed the hours quietly alone with his drink and the piano up in the Theatre Room. Glenda – who had stepped aside as the crowd surged into a mob and let them go, having no desire to witness the outcome, watching the bedlam from a stranger's stoop – cleaned the kitchen in back with Mather. Chesley Sutherland was nowhere around, most likely out working the town feverishly and enthralled.

Haycraft bit at the quiet; he could not be stymied. Overjoyed to see Lambret skulk down the steps into the dining room well after the over-twenty-one policy took effect, he immediately latched onto his protégé and launched into the ramifications of this most recent event. Being a grand believer that no incident was ever isolated, that every action down to going out of one's way to step on a roach creates a net of coincidence throughout the world, he saw omen and metaphor and cultural trend in Old Towne's unnerving afternoon. The shattered windows and strewn trash (*to think they even used the objects we had glorified!*), the broken stoplights flashing red in lapsed alarm, the black crows stomping among deli meats thrown past crumbled curbsides – all signified the larger problem of the low beating against the confines of their impotence. One would have thought it happened at the center of the world, to hear Haycraft speak of it.

— And the plywood boards over our windows here, said Haycraft, I can't think of a more heartbreaking sight. We've had to shut ourselves off from the whole neighborhood. Bunkered ourselves in from the rest of the world.

— Those are going to stay up, Beau answered, indicating the new addition to the room's mishmash décor. Get used to it, Hay. We can't afford new windows. We need the insurance money for other things. Let everyone remember they went at us when we hadn't done anything. And what were you up to out there? I saw you with the bullhorn.

The statement underscored the constrained mood of the

night. Even Haycraft could only move his mouth soundlessly for several long minutes, his mouth like an engine that needed to keep working, grinding out the motions until the words came again. Eventually they did.

— I understand the impulse, he continued. Beau, I *do* understand. I was trying to keep them focused, in a way.…

Beau ignored him, settling on a stool by the broom closet behind the bar and watching the television until someone needed another round. Over one shoulder he said:

— Lambret, it's after ten o'clock, and I do not see you here.

Haycraft pulled the boy away to relative shadows.

— What evades me is why we take out our frustration on what is our own, rather than what is against us. It's irrational to flail blindly and stab our own hands. This neighborhood is our home. Look at what they've done to their own home (Haycraft gestured at the plywood bandages without looking over) – would any sane person do this to their own living room? I was only trying to show how a little ingenuity on their part could bring about change. The golden wastebaskets, you know. I would think if they had felt the need to use them so destructively that they would smash the windows of a government building, not here. It makes as much sense as scarring your own face.

Hay's House of Representatives was being called to order; anyone paying attention could see that. Lambret was the only one paying attention.

— We owe Beau and Glenda something, Hay said. We are at fault here.

Lambret asked what he meant by *we*, as he himself had nothing to do with the riot at all, but had been sleeping back at home on Hay's couch.

— Precisely the wrong attitude! Old Towne is yours, too, you are a part of it, don't you understand? It's a mistake to bother with separations into we and they, when the most applicable point of view would be ours; *us*. It's not so difficult to imagine yourself in the roles of others, Haycraft asserted. Imagination rules the world after all, as much as violence does.

Lambret did not seem convinced.

— Well then at least I am willing to plead guilty to a degree here, Haycraft said. And I owe Beau and Glenda so much.

The short conversation – much of it laden in heavy silences and moody ellipses – led directly to "The Neighborhood Home," one of Hay's favorite editorials ever to appear in *The Old Towne Fair Dealer*. Writing of the willful destruction of the neighborhood by its own inhabitants, he pressed his point that the healthy mind does not do such things to its own habitat, and hit upon his favorite theme: the loss of community. *Contemporary tendencies have distanced the notion of home, hearth, and family*, he wrote. Although he could not imagine any systematic method for doing so, he insisted that a rebuilding of that notion must be undertaken. He took the argument a step further by concluding that *the community itself* had to make up for this uprooted modern family, providing a wider sense of Home. Community: family as adopted strangers. The male characteristics of competition, sullen individuality, and ego assertion had caused these problems, Haycraft argued, and society needed to strengthen the old feminine ideal of welcoming. *A new community hearth is needed*, he insisted. He attacked the gentrified blocks of Old Towne, where the houses appeared as secure as prisons, using them as a general metaphor for this decayed sense of neighborly spirit:

> No more living hidden behind stately barricades! Let us do away with the shutters and blinds, let's put our living rooms out where everyone can share. Old Towne, I urge you to set your sofas on the street!

It made for a beautiful essay, even if Romeo called it a "dismasted rant of utopian fiction." Haycraft was awfully proud of the work.

It was the only time he had written an essay in a single sitting, necessary schedules be damned.

Not that many heard or heeded his call. His *Fair Dealer* was a typical throwaway among many papers in the city – except Hay's effort appeared in smeary blue-ditto print, without graphics. But for a boy such as Lambret, the editorial seemed as important and stirring as anything by the country's founding fathers. He kept at Haycraft to turn the words into action, somehow. *People respond more to what they see than what they read,* he told Hay. *Just like the gold junk. Prove your argument so everyone can find out for themselves.*

Haycraft could be a good listener to any point of view that agreed with his own. Though it meant another break in his schedule, the urgency of his plan called for it, and he was brave. When his next state check arrived, Haycraft cashed it with Glenda at the register (she, understanding already the inevitable unfolding of his designs, immediately put out the tip jar on the corner of the bar). He and Lambret set forth in Beau's clattering pickup to the Daughters of American Veterans consignment shop, made a number of purchases from the furniture floor, and then passed the rest of a Saturday shuttling back and forth between the D.A.V. and the alley behind the Don Quixote. There on the sloped cobblestones the pair arranged a makeshift living room fifty yards long, stocked with sofas, coffee tables, and some of the ugliest lamps imaginable: lamps made from bowling pins, mannequin legs, ceramic monstrosities and long-dead clocks. Lacking electricity, they discarded the shades and lit candles in place of lightbulbs, casting a campfire glow between the avenues.

Immediately they sought out Mather, installed him on a sofa with his art tools, and set him to singing. Lambret corralled his stray dogs and combed them clean. Haycraft called out to whomever happened to pass by to *come on in and sit a spell.* He filled a large fiberglass cooler with iced tea and placed red plastic cups on the coffee table above it – strangers were expected to grab a cup and thrust it through the tea and hang out to get to know their neighbors. If anyone wanted a stronger drink, the Don Quixote was of strategic significance, mere steps away.

Beau and Glenda smiled and said nothing. The community living room did increase foot traffic to the Don Q, after all. Over the initial several days people appeared reluctant to enter (imagine the impact of first sight: Haycraft the bipolar bear in ski cap and suspenders and sandals, watch circled through a belt loop, waving to strangers to join him beside the google-eyed scad Mather Williams, who sang at full-lung the blues of being lost somewhere in the northeast suburbs. Off to one side crouched Romeo with his perpetual manila envelope, on the back of which he took the odd moment to scribble things he would have liked to say to Anantha). People looked once; they stopped; they hurried away with quickened steps. But it was the end of summer, and there was laughter. Here in an alleyway pedestrians found something never seen before. In a few days, people were stopping in and saying they could stand a cold drink of iced tea, all right. Strangers were learning they were next-door neighbors, Lambret's strays were licking the boots of new owners, and Haycraft was shaking hands with the people.

§

— The boy is my delight, Haycraft announced to Beau.

He was responding to the happy sight of several unfamiliar faces dining at the tables behind him – faces heralding money brought to the Don Q, due to his living room in the alley out back. Haycraft Keebler, introducer of common friendliness to the alleys of Old Towne. He credited Lambret for urging him to act on his editorial, and for helping him cart the furniture and set it in a welcoming way. Even now the teenager was outside, languishing on a couch with strangers and a book rather than meeting the men in Frederick Park.

— The boy has promise, Beau, don't you think?

Beau leaned his elbows on the tiled bar, his bald skull shining in the overhead light and showcasing a few age spots among the gray and yellow curly hair that graced his crown and bridged his ears. He shut his eyes tight against the word *promise*.

— The boy is my legacy, Haycraft continued.

— The boy is a hustler, Hay, Beau answered.

He raised his glasses off his bulbous nose and rubbed the bridge of bone there, hard.

— We do not choose the obscurity of our origins…. Lambret is simply the logical consequence of the dire age our community endures. In fact he has thrived with intelligence and distinction despite no family influence, and despite his career as a *hustler* – your term – though I prefer to address him simply as Lamb. My little lamb. He is my light, Beau, and these are dark times.

Beau nodded faintly, accustomed to but wary of Haycraft's grandiloquent moments. Usually they formed the prelude to a manic episode, and Hay had been relatively level for some time (because of the boy? he wondered), working earnestly on his projects. Projects that invariably fatigued him, and therefore the man was due.

— I'm not thinking of him as your light, Hay, I'm thinking of him, period. Glenda and I talk about these things, you know. What are you going to do with the kid? What about school, when's the last time he even went?

— He studies what he wants, vigorously, answered Hay. And he does go to school, sometimes. He has difficulty in math.

— But what can he do with that? You want to help the kid, what's he going to do without school? We're talking about a kid's life, man….

Haycraft left, scuttling up the steps to the door leading outside, and stuck his head out for a brief instant. Then, just as quickly, he darted back to his stool and the topped-off pint Beau already had waiting for him.

— Everything is fine; he is doing quite well.

He paused for a gulp of beer, wiped foam from his mustache.

— But why is everyone so concerned about our Lambret so suddenly? You say you and Glenda discuss such things; there are plenty of others here to cause you anxiety. I have my worries, too. For example, has anyone noticed changes in Mather? Am I the only one disturbed by what I see in his new drawings?

— What, what's wrong with Mather, he's fine, he's singing, Romeo piped in.

— You haven't noticed anything different in his works since Maxwell Hayden was shot?

Romeo dismissed the question with a wave of his hand; he said he had not noticed any changes. When Mather showed him a new work, Romeo glanced over it and murmured approving sounds and that was all that seemed required of him to satisfy the would-be artist; he did not have to specifically examine and critique each new picture. They all looked the same to him anyway. Haycraft was more attentive to subtle changes. He ascended the stairs to the foyer again and came back with a handful of new images Mather had taped to the walls there. Inspecting each one closely, silently, his glasses lowered so he could peer over their frames, he then passed each to Romeo for his own perusal, the heavy construction-bond paper bending over their drinks. Haycraft began pointing out the differences he saw between these and the older pictures on the walls.

— Note the heavy, dark lines, as if he's attacking the paper, he said. And no more gas-station logos or anything like that, he doesn't appear to see anything but faces and fists....

It was true, the pictures were different. They depicted huge heads and angry faces, an emphasis on teeth and tongues, whereas the small bodies below were drawn in little more than wavering traces of outline. Haycraft pointed out that Mather was no longer writing his thoughts, either. Maybe Mather's witnessing of the small riot weeks before had upset the man more than anyone realized. Statement made, Haycraft sat back on his stool, smiling satisfied.

Romeo was not convinced.

— He's got a lot to be angry about, Amanda freaking abandoned him. I can't keep the guy from getting upset, Hay, that's the way life is.

— I would just like to avoid any future violence, countered Haycraft. May I remind you of a certain night when he mistook his broom for a credible lance.

— Look, you worry about your boy and I'll worry about mine, Romeo said, and laughed. I'm the man, I take care of everything.

— How either one of you guys takes care of anyone mystifies me, Beau added, laughing too. Just goes to show there are people out there in a whole world of hurt. And I thought I had it bad.

The comment filled Romeo with glee, and he delved into Wink McCormack and Tyrone Jeffers with shaking antics, upsetting the two mild drunks they were on. But Haycraft set his glass down with unsteady firmness of hand and frowned, unamused. A hoarse vibration thrummed in his throat and he appeared to be thinking. Once his thinking stopped, he turned away from the gathered giggling drinkers and hurried up the steps, opened the door beneath the turning windmill – dodging his head once to avoid a dragging sail – then, just as quickly, darted back to his stool and the topped-off pint Beau had left waiting for him. He did not sit down. To Beau's increasing consternation, he began his ramblings again, now interrupting his spoken thoughts on the boy's wealth of promise and the ramifications of the neighborhood-home's success with short, nervous, humming melodies. Beau thought he recognized "Annie Get Your Gun." Hay's hands, swollen with soft fat, twittered by his glass – a bad sign.

Haycraft's public living room gave the Don Q a leg up on foot traffic, but Beau wanted Hay to go manic somewhere else –

somewhere he could not start a political chat with these new faces; where he would not suddenly begin hauling library books from his satchel and pressing them upon stunned strangers. He tried to fasten the man's attention, and asked what Lambret could be up to tonight.

— He's outside in the hearth, mmmhmmmm, Haycraft told him. Come, come see, Beau. You can afford a minute, no? Look, look look look....

Already Haycraft was in full stride up the stairs, feet attacking the steps with the same insistent purpose as he would have in hot pursuit of some panicked purse snatcher, one hand trailing behind, waving invitation to Beau to follow. With a frown and curse, Beau scuttered up after him in the wake of air left behind, quietly urging him to calm down.

— Look there, Beau Stiles, look at the heathen ragamuffin you all seem to be so concerned about.

They stood in the doorway, Haycraft pushing with one hand the steel bar that freed the lock, using it to lean against the jam. The windmill creaked and swayed above them, cutting through a scene both absurd and alarming. Because of the wood fence closing off the garden from the alleyway, they could see only heads; voices bounced off the brick wall of the opposite building, forming a chamber echo, a feel of the theater after hours. Low murmur of voices in conversation, Mather's tenor soaring over the rest in song. A guitar played softly, perhaps on a porch nearby; it did not match Mather's lyrics or melody. They saw the faces of sad bearded men, a handful with heads back and mouths open in sleep; they saw a woman of brandished burgundy hair, a neighborhood girl scouting the corridor for a hopeful john. Lambret was the most fully visible of everyone, seated on the back of a sofa beside a graded column of burning candles, his face burrowed deep in a book cradled in both hands. The entire alleyway was washed from above in the incandescence of high motion-sensor lamps installed at either end. A bizarre tableau, a contemporary update of an ancient Greek symposium, peopled by ratty street-souls.

— You see? Haycraft pointed out. He wants to learn, my Lamb does. I tutor him to the utmost of my excuse-me-but-I-must-say considerably radical abilities, and I find it as surprising as you but he does respond.

The low hum returned, rising from the bottom of his throat.

— What I'm worried about is trouble, you know ... the two of you together, whatever it is you do. He *is* a minor....

Beau looked back over his shoulder and scanned what he could of his restaurant.

— Not all laws are of proper use to a healthy society! In principle, yes, the issue that worries you is worthy but wouldn't you agree, Beau Stiles? Wouldn't you agree that this is a special case! This is an example of good, and the law – laws need amendments, need rewording, they need to be rectified, I, – a new platform is currently under devise in my head, by the way, where much progress has been made and once the proper advancement and structure of argument is complete shall be launched upon the world. Or at least this city. Launched in a manner that shall seem edifying rather than intimidating to our rather intolerant, ahhhhm, *civic conscience*....

The quiet steps and gentle touch of Glenda caused Haycraft to shout in alarm; he fell into the door with a crash, deranging the wood blinds that covered the window. It caused him to lose his thread of thought and he turned almost violently at her, his eyes large behind thick lenses, flashing fear.

— It's just me, Haycraft, she soothed, gently massaging the thick of his shoulder. *Shhhh.*

At the sight of her, at the sound of her clement voice, Haycraft settled immediately with an audible sigh. His posture eased, and the bend to the wood blinds corrected itself behind him.

— A perfect example of the philosophy proposed in my best editorials, Hay spoke again. For whoever shall read them, which, at the moment and to my distress, I fully believe to be Lamb and a handful of others equally lacking in influence. Compassion. Security. *Glenda*. You know what I am going to say, Beau: Imagine the strides we could make if our government, our markets, reflected your wife's genial face? She is the *yes* of Molly Bloom....

Glenda squeezed his shoulder somewhat harder.

— I want you to calm down, Haycraft. Lower your voice. It's all very nice what you're saying, and maybe true, but you have to remember this is a public place and there are many people here whom we don't know well tonight, and you don't know what they are thinking or what they do. Until you change the laws you must abide by them.

— Be human first, a subject later! Respect not the law, but what is right!

Shhh, both Glenda and Beau urged at once. With the unspoken agreement peculiar to long-married couples, they moved in unison, synchronized; Beau took Haycraft's arm and led him out another few steps beyond the trailing sails of the windmill as Glenda reached for the steel bar and pulled the door shut behind her.

And Haycraft understood. He nodded to Beau and spoke more quietly, gazing at the gallows swing of the blinds behind the door's window, focusing there as though he could peer through to Glenda's form moving quietly back into the restaurant to chat with the guests.

— No less a lover of truth than Thoreau said that any man more right than his neighbors constitutes a majority of one. Lamb and I, together, make a majority of two. *Ten people who speak make more noise than ten thousand who are silent.* Napoleon said that. It is sad how people prefer to speculate on personal scandals rather than on the daily scandals of public life.... Oh, that's a good one there. Worthy of exploration and explication, that one right there, make a mental note. I tell you, Beau, my finger is pressed hard, *dug in,* on the pulse of the times and our people.

He trailed off and set to humming again, his eyes on the head-bowed, studious boy.

— What a voracious appetite he has! Just look at him, Beau, he blurted again. I tell you he is both son and companion to me, two things you know as well as anyone that I have never had and have always longed for.

Beau did as told: He looked, hoping the moment would pass and Haycraft would calm down and they could both go back to join the others at their usual stations at his bar, where their concerns could fall again to issues prompted by the TV and nothing of more pertinent value. But what he saw only certified what must have been a growing feeling that this night would be a long night, and not good for business: Over the spiked planks of the garden fence he saw Lambret's eyes shut in the same beat as the muffled thump of a book closed. The boy leaned his head back against the brick and gently pushed a long stray lock of black hair behind his ear. He appeared to be taking a rest, perhaps contemplating whatever passage he had finished – Haycraft was explaining the boy was on to Emerson now but was having difficulties with the baroque structure of nineteenth-century sentences, "so nimble with commas" – even as one arm apparently sought out an object not seen because of the wood fence. The arm groped; it reached; the boy's eyes opened, and then both hands were at work out of sight.

They watched as the hand appeared with a rag, and the rag fastened over the mouth, and his eyes closed dreamily. Lambret inhaled a deep breath. His head lounged back against the brick, and the eyes seemed to filter slowly open again, staring off toward the darkening sky.

— Ah, damn it all to hell, Haycraft, Beau spat.

— I make no claim of understanding. An addiction –

— Get him out of here, he can't do that shit in front of my club!

— Perhaps we should push him toward De Quincey, I should get him *Confessions of an English Opium Eater*....

But Beau was no longer listening; he was moving to shout at the boy, bringing both hands to cup his mouth. Before he made any sound Haycraft's own hands had covered his and all Beau managed was a muffled grunt, a falling into Hay's body, Hay's voice in his ear whispering fraught, intense phrases that veered from *Be quiet* to *I'm sorry Beau* and *Hold on listen*.

— Give me a few minutes to take care of it myself. No need for shouting or scenes. He has a delicacy –

— Take care of it now, Beau interrupted him, reaching his hand to the handle of the door, his thumb resting on the brass latch. Get the kid out of here and you know what, maybe you should just go on home, too. Jesus, clear out, the both of you. Give me and Glenda a break tonight, why don't you? How long do you people expect us to put up with this shit?

The words shot from over the shoulder of the Hawaiian-print shirt as Beau turned fully away from him, headed for the door. Haycraft stood dumbly at the sense these words made, uncertain if he had heard Beau Stiles, his good lifelong friend, correctly. He blinked behind the thick lenses of his glasses, mouth open; he had no response. To think Beau of all people would shun him because of what he found in the boy. Above all things, a question of the heart. The heart's wishes against the expectations of loved ones. An editorial in that. There was an excellent editorial in that one there. Haycraft could let his thoughts and opinions be clearly known to all of them then, once he had the time to calm himself, to straighten his thoughts (they seemed to fly through him now, half-thoughts launching into others, into impressions and yes, even sensations such as the heat on his face and neck, the scabrous heat of the dying day, and colors, a pulsing blue and flickering red, a staccato beat in the air around him). The tick of the windmill tricked Haycraft's eyes into looking up at the sails turning slowly, the dark of one long staff shadowing an arc against the deep twilight blue of the late summer sky. Deep twilight, almost night, his favorite hour (the peacocks in Tennessee, their beautiful lonesome squalls), and when did night ever fully begin? He and Lambret had discussed that topic just the other day, about how difficult it was to mark distinctly between the two, day and night, how night seemed to be so much more clearly delineated than day, yet how difficult it was to clearly pinpoint one apart from the other – here daytime stops, and night has begun. If the sun in summer set at 9:27 PM, then one could assert that night began at 9:28, yet you only had to look to see that the sun's last rays still cast rose light over all, therefore, day. Yet if you were to mention to someone else what you were doing at 8:30 you would say, *Last night I....* How unfathomably odd.

Perhaps he had already been looking at the windmill and only the tick and creak of the axle jolted him from his thoughts strongly enough to register the thing before him. Full night had fallen, strengthening the colors before him again, snapping the sails from red to blue, freezing them in brief instants of motion, as when one tries to follow a single blade of a spinning fan, dizzying the eyes. But why red? Why blue?

Haycraft spun from the entrance and looked toward his alley-way living room. The brick walls throbbed with colored lights, the vascular colors so often recognized on those streets, the flashes pushed to the wall by the strong white cone of light streaking the length of the alley. Chesley Sutherland strode past the fence in blue uniform as two colleagues started into demands for identification from the gathered, sleepy-stirring men. The crackle of radios fought above shouts and the guttering drone of idling engines. Haycraft ran down the steps and through the garden as fast as his sandals would allow; he hurled himself at the gate, but due to his agitation and the curse of his clumsy hands it took several moments to open the resistant lock. He fought; he kicked; by the time the latch gave way and he stood in the alley, he was face-to-face with a smiling Chesley Sutherland.

— Exactly the man I wanted to speak to, Chesley said. I read the signature of a Keebler shenanigan all over this mess. Hay, what are you up to here?

A short row of disheveled souls stood lined against the wall, their faces creased with grimy wrinkles of worry, shuffling through their patched pockets or else making gestures of mis-understanding to the officers interrogating them. A quick survey gave no sign of Lambret. Haycraft scanned the rest of the area quickly, up and down the length of the alleyway that tremored with each beat of the police lights, but he saw no one. A quart of porch sealant lay on its side at the foot of a tattered, fungal sofa; the aluminum can flexed in coughlike spasms as it spilled into a widening skirt, slowly soaking the foundation beneath the brick wall, the only clue – hopefully, a clue to Haycraft only – that Lambret had ever been there.

He was pleased to find Chesley was not looking at him. Sutherland was inspecting the neighborhood living room, the dowdy couches and splintering coffee tables, the ludicrous lamps. It stank of the chemical spill. He motioned over it all with his flashlight, taking in the scene with the same look of resigned disappointment as a football coach watching his team perform far below expectations. A look not of surprise, but of an avoided suspicion confirmed.

— You got to clear all this crap out of here, Hay. It's not good.

— Clear it out? This is a local gathering place for *neighbors* –

— Neighbors, yeah. Nah, it's blocking the alley, see. Can't do that. You got to get it out of here. We need to keep the pathways clear. Deliveries and all that.

The humming returned to Haycraft's throat; his mouth worked at his teeth. His hands slapped at his thighs as he started into an odd gait, one that circled briefly away from Chesley before turning back again.

— These alleys have been blocked for decades and no one cared; we only had them emptied after, after....

— After what? Chesley interrupted, smiling, his flashlight now bent upward to Haycraft's face, forcing the man again through his strange circle of steps, his thigh slaps. You have something to tell me, Hay? You didn't have anything to do with all that gold-painted junk in the alleys a while back, did you? You didn't do anything to make that bus crash, did you?

Haycraft could not get out any words, only that frustrated hum and mutter, his mouth opening and closing silently as a silent fish that stares from behind aquarium glass, seemingly frightened and unconcerned at once. Chesley moved the light away, used the butt of the grip to raise his cap brim so that it no longer tucked low over his eyes.

— Look Hay, it's my job. There's been a complaint.

— A complaint? From whom? Who would complain about such obvious improvements?

Chesley did not have the chance to answer. A ruckus in the alley distracted them both. At the far end came a clatter, then shouts; the other officers were having difficulties. With a curse Sutherland set off, Haycraft following, both men jogging to catch up and find an agitated Mather Williams spinning between two officers, then three, his curled fingers revealing strikingly long fingernails.

You do not touch me you leave me alone, Mather cried. *You do not touch me I am so sorry I can fix it.*

Sutherland called his name once, twice, but Mather did not answer – he slashed his hands in the air before him, crouched and ready to pounce. His eyes were narrowed and feline, squinched tight against the flashlights.

— Be careful, he doesn't like to be touched by strangers, Haycraft offered.

An officer laughed at the obvious point made. Three of them circled warily around Mather, not daring to near him yet, not really wanting a tussle.

The upset intrigued Haycraft only briefly. In this pause he saw a perfect opportunity to return to what he considered the heart of the matter – a complaint of some formal nature being made against the alleyway living room. He tugged at Chesley's elbow to keep his focus on the matter at hand. What complaint? Who complained? Chesley yanked his arm from Haycraft without looking; instead he spoke to Mather Williams, reintroducing himself as the man who used to keep the Don Q safe at night, reminding Mather as best he could (*You remember me, don't you? Remember how you always told me to have a blessed night?*); he spoke in calming tones as he neared, his mag light gone and both hands raised so Mather could see them.

— We don't want any trouble, he said.

— You don't need to be worried, Haycraft added then, in response to which Chesley did turn and asked if Haycraft could get the man out of there.

— I've no idea, Haycraft answered. Perhaps the best thing would be to leave him alone, perhaps if you left there would be no problem here at all.

Mather, in his turn, only backed onto the seat of the couch behind him, crouching there, his large eyes rolling. *Do not close in on me Mr. Sutherland,* he shouted. *Yes I remember who you are you know I got nothing to do like my cousin.*

Nothing the policemen did made the slightest difference; it was a standoff. At each hesitation Haycraft continued to niggle at Chesley's back, demanding a name to attach to the complaint against him.

— Surely it's nothing more than a misunderstanding, reasoned Haycraft, Someone feels left out and does not realize that the entire community was invited.

— Hay, you have to let me deal with this right now. We will talk in a minute, Chesley ground out through bared teeth, his jaw clenched and thickened hard, making a line perpendicular to the brim of his cap.

Mather, he began, nearing the man again, and now it was

Romeo rushing up from behind them all, shouting to Mather to just hold on, he was coming, he was there. He pushed past Haycraft and Sutherland, placing himself between the officers and Mather. *Why didn't you come get me?* he fumed. Then, speaking softly, he told Mather that everything was all right – that Romeo was there, that he would take care of everything. And gradually the fierce look in Mather's face softened; he allowed his eyes to move from his assailants to the more comfortable vision of his friend Romeo, who stepped closer. *I didn't do anything wrong,* Mather said; *I know,* Romeo answered. *Come down from the sofa, no one is going to hurt you.*

Mather looked at his hands, and they transformed from the pointed claws to soft hands again. He straightened himself on the sofa, the small man now standing nearly straight, head inclined and eyes downcast. It made another odd tableau for the evening, the policemen gathered around in the throbbing light, their flashlights illuminating white circles on the ground; Mather Williams standing on his sofa as though on a stage, frozen there above them.

He stepped down to the cobblestones. The drift of officers soughed to one another with smiles of relief, a touch of embarrassment. Romeo put his arm around Mather and turned him away from them, from their lights, as Mather railed to him over how he had just been singing, he was doing what he was supposed to and singing when these police come up and tell him he was causing trouble. Romeo walked him away, slowly, agreeing with everything he said, apologizing for not being there when the emergency occurred. He suggested they go for a ride somewhere in his car.

Haycraft broke into the brief calm, immediately accosting Chesley over the meaning of it all:

— Do you see what kind of disturbance you've caused? I thought you were sworn to uphold order!

— Keebler, just get the stuff out of here now and forget about it, all right? You're the one at the heart of this, and you got nobody here but a bunch of bums and crazies.

— Tell me who has complained, let me speak with them, doesn't the accused have the right to face his accusers? Not one person has said a thing to me and even Beau admits it has helped his business –

— Get it out of here, Chesley repeated. I should write a citation is what, listen I like you and Beau's on this alley too so he'd get dragged into it and you and I both know he doesn't need any troubles. Just get the stuff out of here, okay?

But Haycraft had stuck on the subject of complaint. He wanted to know who had called the police without first speaking to him about any disturbance his neighborly idea might have caused; he was certain he could have convinced said person to see the error in such complacent, reactionary judgment. He stamped his foot; he would not allow Sutherland to interrupt him until he had finished. He raised his hands in plaintive outrage at what he could not help but allow to impress him as personal insult and injustice. He spoke of petitions and walkouts, marches on city hall (*It will be Maxwell Hayden all over again!*); he declared he could take his own complaint into the mayor's office himself.

None of which surprised or affected Chesley Sutherland. The exchange between them ended with the flashing lights darkened and drawn away in the engine churn of American-made patrol cars, Haycraft clutching a city citation against his chest, and Sutherland's last words echoing in his head: *You tell your kid I saw him run. I want these streets clean, Haycraft Keebler. You tell him to keep running; I like it that way.*

§

Haycraft did not see Lambret again that night. Nor did he hear from him over the next ten days. A discombobulating scenario for the man, as he needed as little disturbance and change as possible to keep his head clear and his mouth shut, and the neighborhood-home fiasco had provided enough agitation to last him some time. He asked Beau to cart away the furniture in his truck before the Don Quixote opened for the hoped-for lunch crowd that rarely came, and in the midst of the move convinced his keeper to allow him use of his front yard to sell off the pieces for any price he could get. A complete usurpation of his weekend, one that set him to mutterings and curses and long perplexing silences, to weird hand gestures that sprang in midwalk, none of which helped offset the monetary losses from buying the D.A.V. furniture. Such events were portents, he informed Beau; further proof that for no action of his own he'd been assigned a place in the underbelly of history.

— Perhaps I did terrible things in a previous life, he said, sadly.

It made for Don Q nights stretched long and lonely for Haycraft, then for nights stretched long and lonely at home, as he could not find the energy to leave. The door leading out of his apartment became the door to all his problems and failures, the door that led to a life of payback for what may have been the selfish one previous.

At first Haycraft believed his body required only a good rest after all the activism of the past several months, the cajoling work his destiny demanded; but he knew himself well, too. He had been tipping the high end of his psychological spectrum and halving the Lithium and Zyprexa almost nightly with Glenda, whose uninsured buckshot nerves required soothing. Now, with the boy absent, he recognized the old struggles waxing before him, the constant muddle, Keebler fuming over his own short-comings and the boy's – the boy who disappeared.

Haycraft had learned that smoking could sometimes help, when he feared he was bottoming out. He was a man who lived by signs and symbols, however, and merely taking the walk to the nearest convenience store for a carton of all-natural, additive-free cigarettes proved debilitating; it showed he was losing. He would walk into the store and find he had forgotten why he had come; an hour would pass roaming the aisles, and it wouldn't be until he had decided to leave that he would spot the cartons stacked behind the counter, and remember. Pulling rumpled bills from his pocket he would notice the shaking hands – another awful signature of what was happening to him, as he could hardly recognize these hands as his own – and then find himself in consternation at the stutter that prevented his asking for the blasted carton; he had to give up and simply point at what he wanted. Outside, the day's brightness assailed him as a hopeless beacon, granting him none of the boost sunlight usually gave.

At home it could require another good hour to remove a pack from the carton, to corral a dirty plate as ashtray, only to realize then that he had not had the presence of mind to ask for lighter or matches. Thus he was forced to situate himself in the kitchen near the stove – another process of arrangement that took much longer than the act required. The gas burners frightened him. Haycraft just knew if he held the cigarette by his lips and leaned into the flame it would be at the precise moment the gas would surge through the line, resulting in an incendiary burst that would devour his mustache, his face; he would be left with a wad of bubbled flesh for a nose, perhaps blind. To avoid this, he held the cigarette to the flame by hand, not inhaling, furthering the whole ritual which now seemed abject and pointless. But he knew the cigarettes would help and so pushed through, sitting in the old school desk, each inhalation drawn deeply with a quiet sough, each exhalation only adding to his sense of depletion.

During these times he would not sleep. He would remain in the chair for hours, propping his feet on the windowsill, taking them down again, his eyes scraping against the confines of his skin, his soul sinking into sordid lassitude. During these times he could not eat, instead filling himself with coffee and water, grateful for the action drinking allowed. His House of Representatives disappeared: Simple urges and decisions, such as when it had become necessary to go to the bathroom – had, in fact, suddenly become unavoidable and required instant movement – transformed into demanding acts of will. His body *needed to go*, yet he felt ambivalent about it. He hated it when these times befell him; he hated himself for having to endure them; yet they also gave him a sense of sad comfort, in the same way a man might return to the family that had once betrayed and rejected him, releasing himself to the embrace of people he knew he could not trust.

§

Eventually Glenda pulled him from the apartment and ensconced him again at his rightful place in the Don Quixote. *You are only allowed to sulk a few days,* she said, *then you return to where I can see you.* It was a kind of agreement they shared, a way of looking out for one another. She grabbed some books messed over the folding desk chair, led him to the pickup, drove in silence with the radio on and then marched him to his booth, where she sat Haycraft down and stood a moment over him, hands on her hips.

— I strive to be agreeable, said Haycraft.

Glenda served his beer and otherwise left him alone, allowing Hay to give himself over to listless wonderings of when would the dear Lamb appear again, hours passing over stale half-downed pints and the short stack of books at his office-booth. The subjects ranged now over the lives of saints, the "desert fathers" (*Take away temptations and no one will be saved*), Augustine's *Confessions*. He liked to play a game with Augustine's book, so pious to the point of exasperation, every sentence beginning or ending to the Glory of God Who Made All Things Possible. Haycraft liked to replace the omnipresent word *God* in the text with anything else that happened to strike his fancy. *Argument*: "Let the haughty laugh at me, let them laugh who have never yet been flat on their faces, felled for their own good by you, my Argument." *Ale*: "It was not out of reverence for your purity that I rejected this evil thing, O Ale of my heart...." A game Lambret would appreciate, perhaps even like, a game he would make much more inventive than Haycraft ever could, with that youthful point of view, often too clever for his own good. Hay alone with his sighs, glancing around the room empty save Romeo drinking alone, his hand lazing over the manila envelope that accompanied him every-where since Anantha left, covered now with the hurried scrawl of a man discovering important points he did not have the pres-ence of mind to make during their earlier, final discussions. A scattering of musicians at the bar watched a baseball game and discussed matters of the pennant race, always between teams far away from Montreux. They waited hopefully, and then less hope-fully, for anyone to arrive, in order to start their set in the Theatre Room upstairs. Mather Williams clanked pans in the kitchen behind the slatted saloon doors and sang to Glenda.

Over a week away from the boy and Hay was desperate. He made a lament to Romeo in just that way, *Romeo, I'm desperate,* such a degree of frailty in the hoarse croak of his voice and wavering tremors of hands that even Romeo was touched by his longing. He bought Haycraft a beer: the quickest method of commiseration he understood. As a way of slower, deeper solace, he spoke:

— It's the kid that's the trouble, Hay. If you had a woman you'd know this mood wouldn't last.

— I have no idea what you are talking about, Haycraft said.

— You've got your philosophies, I've got mine. Hear me out at least. See, with the boy what you've got going isn't real natural, that's my view. It forces you to reinvent the wheel, as it were. You take care of him, you all do whatever it is you all do, and that's that. And the odds of you finding another boy someday are extremely long –

Haycraft straightened his thick shoulders and raised his head with sudden indignity, ready to speak, but Romeo held up his hand to stop him.

— Hear me out. You don't have to agree. But see, women are everywhere and they're always on the lookout. You lose one and you feel bad about it and then after some time another comes along. And women, they look out for their guy whether they want to or not. You need looking out for. A woman likes you, she does these little things that, I can't explain it really, these little things that make life easier, make you feel better about yourself. Something as simple as the way she looks at you when you walk in the door. And I'm not even talking yet about sex –

— Is this really a conversation you need to have with me? Haycraft asked.

— You are halfway there already, that's all I'm saying, the boy's half-skirt as it is, continued Romeo. But *a woman*, Hay. You got a hard life, and women are all solace. They're not as easy as a guy to get along with sometimes, true. But you get that back in the sex. You fight, and you fuck it right again. I don't see how you can do that with the kid. I *don't want* to think about you doing that with the kid.

— Romeo, these are most interesting ideas, said Haycraft thoughtfully. I also disagree with all of my soul, and believe that you are coming off as more of a bastard than even I allowed before. To even suggest –

— No one says truth is a pretty sight, man. I think my point of view here comes from evolutionary thinking, propagation of the species, urges we can't rationally comprehend, stuff like that.

— Yes. I understand irrational urges. Why don't I chalk up this discussion as one of them, on your part. I can see by the scrawl all over your envelope there, and the sight of her name, that you are a man in difficulties and thus have a bit of rage to work through. Which is natural. How is our Anantha?

Anantha had been on her American tour over two months. Despite the number of words consuming the envelope like ants over a discarded picnic sandwich, the contact between them had been confined to notes of postcard depth that arrived with the polaroids of Anantha's performances, sent for Romeo to add to their Web site. In her latest missive she mentioned settling down in Van Nuys, California, because it was the center of the adult film industry. *This is where all that money is,* she wrote.

— If there is one place in the world where I will never live, it is California, Romeo maintained to Beau, to Haycraft.

Not that she had invited him to join her. But Romeo had reached that stage where he needed to convince himself that he just did not care any longer. The point where you announce that *it's the principle of the thing* that bothers you now, not the pain of dashed hopes or the crushed heart confronted long before.

§

That Lambret arrived late the next night, very late when the windmill had stilled in the summer darkness and its sails loomed shadowy against the dull mercury vapor light that swelled the sky bottom, changed much and nothing. It seemed an arrival of provocation, almost. He waited quietly at the top of the steps where Chesley used to stand before rejoining the force, between a ficus tree in perpetual death throes and the bronze head of Cervantes, and took in the scene below, waiting to be noticed. One look at Haycraft was clue enough to know he had passed sufficient time away. He was a resourceful boy and manipulative in the way only adolescents know how to be. He knew he had upset the older man, knew also that there would be arguments and lectures around his continued, hidden huffing; he would have to be chastised for running from the police, and a fraught distance would fall between them – a distance and discomfort he felt no need to deal with. By waiting days before reappearing Lambret knew Hay would be more concerned with urgent reunion than any airing of grievances. Looking at Haycraft bent alone, so absolutely alone in his booth, his face set inches from a text like a mouth open on the table, Lambret knew he had been right.

He moved quietly to Haycraft, and asked a simple question:

— What are you reading now?

Haycraft read aloud: *I polluted the stream of friendship with my filthy desires and clouded its purity with hellish lusts; yet all the while, befouled and disgraced though I was, my boundless vanity made me long to appear elegant and sophisticated.*

He shut *The Confessions* with a snap, let his palm rest over its cover.

— Sit with me, Hay said. I have missed you.

Sit with me, I have missed you being perhaps the most longed-for declaration a boy like Lambret had ever imagined.

§

They accompanied one another in renewed reverie, Haycraft's swollen, hirsute hand draped over Lambret's small, white, frail and hairless one; their feet touched toe to toe beneath the table. Heartened by the boy's reappearance, Haycraft forgot to ask if he would like to play the little reading game of Augustine's pieties; he had forgotten the book altogether, pushing it aside to make room for his elbow on the table so that he could lay his chin in hand to view Lambret without distraction, pushing aside his odd thoughts of what Romeo had had to say the night before. Haycraft simply did not understand the man. He didn't think Romeo understood himself, either. But there was no shame in that.

Lambret noted that Hay had lost a significant amount of weight.

— Yes, I have founded a new diet, Haycraft informed him. Eat nothing but potatoes; they are very rich in iron and are capable of being prepared in a multitude of ways.

Lambret nodded gravely, his face low and serious, his eyes not leaving Hay's.

The answer was a one-off and they let it lie. The silence fell awkwardly, too, as neither could discover what next to say. Augustine's yearning, his sense of life's reappraisal, must have sunk into Haycraft's mood. And maybe Romeo's thoughts had thrown him off balance. He felt he had something important to say but was not sure how to go about it; this was new territory. Once Beau set up Lambret with the "strong drink" the boy liked – soda water mixed with cranberry and orange juice – Haycraft set intent and discerning eyes on the young face. He took in the thin inward curl of that inflamed upper lip, the intermittent sniffles that never cleared the boy's nasal passages. He looked deeply into Lambret's dark and studious eyes with all the intensity of a rejected lover (with the intensity of a Romeo Díaz bent over his manila envelope, pen in hand), opened his mouth to speak, but instead began his humming. He took off his glasses to wipe his eyes, replaced the glasses again. Lambret sat with an unhurried, listless smile, his mouth weak rather than cruel, as though he were in on a tired joke Haycraft had yet to fathom.

— We have to talk, Haycraft said, and the smile on Lambret's face tightened. We have to talk about the way you live, Haycraft began again. You look awful.

Lambret answered by taking his hand away and running it through the greasy thick of his hair.

— We have to talk about this, Haycraft said again, feeling his way into a conversation that quickly ran down chutes and flumes neither of them had planned or wanted:

We don't have to talk at all, said Lambret, You are not taking proper care of yourself, counseled Haycraft; I don't need you to tell me how to care for myself, I needed a few days off is all, But look at you, when did you last eat? Hay this is how I am and you don't need me trailing around all the time, But you have such dark circles under your eyes, your mouth is chapped painfully dry and I know what that means, Hey I'm all right, Do you know Chesley Sutherland says he's after you, he's a policeman Lamb and this is not a good time for you to be out on the streets.

— What makes you think I was on the streets? You don't think I have other friends, people with houses?

Haycraft did not have a response; he was unprepared for this discussion. He set his hand on Lambret's again as a way of appearing less threatening and interrogating and then just as quickly withdrew, leaning back from Lambret to look over the room surrounding. Beau stood on guard behind the bar and behind Romeo, who had turned halfway on his stool; both men were watching his table, following their conversation. It occurred to Haycraft that the overhead speakers were no longer playing music – why? So they could hear better at the bar? He resented that. He shot them an outraged glare and they quickly occupied themselves with other things: Beau with a washrag, Romeo with his compelling highball. But Haycraft knew he was expected to say certain things this night.

— Tell me why you do it.

— Do what, the boy wanted to know, even if he did know, the both of them knew: the thinner, the spray paint remnants, the butane and rubber cement; even gasoline, despite Lambret's apparent (to Haycraft) intelligence. The bald question was *Why*. *Why* and *How*, the two bedrock words in Haycraft's vocabulary, the two fundamental queries to which he complained he could rarely find answer.

Apparently Lambret could not see a reason to betray that tradition. As if the boy could be expected to explain why anyone chooses to throw themselves aside, away from where they are.

— That is not the issue I am trying to address here. I want to help you, Lamb. I want to help, don't you understand that?

Surely Lambret understood. But he was sixteen, seventeen, hazy-scrambled in the head. One moment he didn't care, the next he cared with the full force of his heart. He cared, he didn't care. He didn't care, he cared too much. It was fucking exhausting, he said.

Haycraft responded only with a steady gaze, a parental face dictating he would not be distracted so easily.

Hay, I don't mean to hurt you.

But Haycraft was hurt. The boy was rotting away before him despite all efforts, a notion that had only grown over his interlude of despondent staring through fogged windows, grazing on fears that Lambret had fallen into real trouble, he was being threatened by someone truly evil, he had lost hope in the possibilities Haycraft wanted to open up for him – all these fears only growing, festering, over his time of solitude. How could he explain this to a teenage boy so that he could understand? How to explain, when this child, quickened by the streets, could only recognize that Haycraft owed him nothing? Haycraft did not know what gesture would prove convincing. He sat there, caught within the casual interest of Beau and Romeo watching him speak from across the room, and the smirk on Romeo's face exposed everything the man was thinking: how ridiculous he found forty-two-year-old Haycraft so distraught with this chicken from the alleyways. How absurd, a lovers' quarrel between man and boy. He remembered Romeo telling him that women were available everywhere, waiting, that he wouldn't find another boy again.

— You do not have to stay with me if you don't wish to, Haycraft said quietly, turning again to Lambret. I am only trying to show you, to show you some light, Lamb. There is no light in a soaked rag.

The humming again; the fluttering of fingers one over another; the twitching knee.

Lambret asked what other books there were on the table.

Haycraft answered by pushing the few books closer. For a few long moments more he sat without speaking, the boy inspecting spines while Hay sat with a stillness forced over his entire body. His head moved slowly from side to side as if trying to clear his mind after suffering a surprised blow. *Well,* he declared, bringing his hands to his knees with a clap. Lambret flipped pages of text his eyes did not read.

Haycraft rose and started across the room; as he moved away he had the impression of crossing a great distance, of passing through a long succession of gates, passing through successive darknesses, the blackest point lying at the table he had left behind. Things were changing, anyone who cared to lend their attention to the matter could see that. At the end of the darkness sat Romeo beneath the glow of bar lights, shiny stars reflecting off the wine glasses hung from a wood trellis above. The thousand reflections and the glass and mirrors made the bar appear set within some kind of strange saloon firmament. Romeo set his hand across the manila envelope as Haycraft approached, moved it aside to make room, without looking. In his other hand he swirled the scotch-ambered ice of his glass.

— Trouble with love? he asked, sharp grin widening as he tilted his head back and tumbled a few shards of ice into his mouth.

— Indeed, Haycraft answered. You mock me but I do not care. Do you know what I'm going to tell you…? I feel the urge to help. It's a compulsion you know and I feel guilty for wanting to help, as though by caring for the boy I've laid a huge burden on him. It's such a difficult thing to understand.

— They always are, Romeo said. Relationships always are.

Haycraft straightened in vivid shock: His hands gripped the mahogany trim of the bar and his eyes saucered huge behind the thick lenses of his glasses. In this pause Romeo turned – a glance – to look at him.

— What?

— That is perhaps the warmest thing you have ever said to me, Romeo. You are not a sympathetic man.

— This is true, Romeo agreed.

— Perhaps you are softening. No, not *softening,* you would take that as a pejorative remark – perhaps *growing...?* All this business with Mather during Anantha's absence, is there a change going on in Romeo Díaz? That was very noble the other night, when you calmed him down. Yes, I sense a palpable change.

— A phase, said Romeo. Don't get used to it.

He exchanged the now-empty glass for a fresh drink from Beau – a difference in habit as usually he insisted he nurse the same glass throughout the night, adding ice and scotch as needed instead of accepting a new glass with each round. Beau swiped the used glass from the counter and immediately got to washing it in the sink beneath the bar, as though he were very busy and had to labor with diligence and efficiency in order to keep the workspace clean.

Romeo was dressed in what the regulars were now calling his Post-Anantha attire: dark sport coat, tie loose at the neck, spangled cuff links shining dully in the bar light. A once-sharp outfit now wrinkled and rumpled, yanked from the hamper and sniffed at the armpits before gracing Romeo's body again. The crimped tie limped down his belly; his face sagged swollen from either lack of sleep or having just awakened; his short hair sprang in unruly shoots. Only a few short months had passed since his failure with Anantha before the camera, and so when he turned now and stared at Lambret through eyes blistered by liquor and smoke, the boy felt his gaze and shifted away, squirming deeper into his book. It wasn't until Glenda arrived behind the bar to speak with Haycraft that Romeo began to ignore the boy again. Glenda leaned over the trim to whisper:

— Hay I'm so wound up tonight, I can't think straight. I see your friend has come back and I do hope this makes you happy. But you wouldn't happen to have any of your good pills on you, would you? For a tired old woman?

— Of course, Glenda, you know whatever I have is yours,

Haycraft said, handing over a prescription bottle. Take a couple of smiles, he added.

— You've lost some weight, haven't you, Hay?

— Potatoes, Haycraft answered, serious and stark-eyed, cheeks drawn in dramatically.

Glenda nodded as though she understood perfectly. She left him then, merging again into the sparse crowd filtering in beneath the sailing windmill outside; into the regular night; into a hundred nights, a thousand. Beau once declared that running the Don Quixote was like listening to an orchestra play the same theme endlessly, with countless tiny variations. The main theme being entirely inconsistent with its original intent. For as obtuse as Haycraft's ideas could appear – that our society, and Old Towne in particular, was in crisis due to a cultural history of striving for the Self-Made Man, a masculine repression of the feminine traits of emotional consciousness and participation with the spirit of the world – the Don Q was fairly designed to embody such ideas; it was to be the locus of the resolution of said ideas: a celebratory atmosphere that recognized the values of partnership, pluralism, the interplay of many perspectives. A place to be imaginative and compassionate, to follow one's intuition as Roseanne Cash and Patsy Cline serenaded from the jukebox until night's end, when the Third World lanterns dimmed and the cash register chimed out the shift's accounting.

What they had was Haycraft Keebler; Romeo Díaz; Mather Williams, and the boy-hustler Lambret Dellinger, who reeked faintly of chemicals. And this night, lit from below by Romeo's strange grin and Haycraft's surprised openness to it, this night the melodic variation on the theme felt darker, exploring an anxious and agitated key.

Lambret dove deep into a book he could not bring himself to read. Glenda and Mather sang lightly together behind the saloon doors, in the kitchen. Haycraft rested a meaty hand on shrunken Romeo's shoulder. He shined contentment and confidence, unexpectedly sudden, like a man who had striven for years to construct a theory no one believed, unifying most everything, and had now been proved correct. As if at that precise instant *it all came together*. As Beau busied himself beneath the bar Hay launched into his vision of the incremental difference between how things should be and how things are, of the sanctity of the bond he shared with the boy and the valuable rarity of that bond; how, together, they were making the act of reading a social affair again, a method of self-improvement; how – oh, he admitted, he could say this only now because Chesley Sutherland was away out patrolling the streets, pursuing his conviction that crimes were occurring at every moment – but together he and Lamb had managed to cleanse the plaque from the arteries of Old Towne. *Golden, shining nuggets*, he beamed, *beauty where there used to be ruins. I, Beau; I and the boy.*

— I didn't care much for the beauty through my window, answered Beau.

He smiled into the silence this caused, softly sucking on a straw in his ceramic stein filled with the habitual rum and cola, the stein stamped with his initials, BS, a pun that tickled him. Romeo sat with his head directed toward the TV, his palm lying flat over the manila envelope. He said nothing. His left leg jerked rhythmically from the ankle, anchored on the steel stays of his bar stool.

— Buy me a drink, Hay, he said, tapping one finger on the rim of an empty glass before him.

— A drink for our Romeo, Beau, wherefore art a scotch for our brokenhearted Romeo! Hay barked.

— I am not brokenhearted, Romeo said. Jesus Christ, brokenhearted is not the word. I dodged a bullet and am thus thankful. She would have been the end of me.

He straightened from the slump he'd been held in before. Haycraft was humming his melodies, not quite listening. When the drink arrived Hay snatched it from the bar and cradled the back of Romeo's head with one free hand, using the other to force the glass to Romeo's lips.

— Drink up, then. Drink to your relief!

Romeo pulled back from the glass and a splash of scotch landed on his throat, soaking quickly into the unbuttoned collar, the greasy tie. He placed his palm over the entire glass rim, pushing it back down with a steady force against Hay's hand. He told Haycraft he would appreciate it were he not to do that anymore. Hay responded with an unfamiliar and doltish laugh.

— Well I for one am brokenhearted, then, if no one else cares to admit it. Amanda – yes, I call her *Amanda*, stage names sound ridiculous to me – Amanda I liked! She was like a fresh beam of light in this foggy old place that smells of … you know, it smells something like pesticide in here. Why is that, Beau? Romeo: Amanda, your Anantha, she was right in a way, she is something of a star, a new kind pointing to the future instead of sending us light that died a thousand years before. She fits my paradigm, in a skewed sort of way. What she does is rather selfless, I think.

— Jesus Christ! Romeo shouted.

Haycraft's fingers fluttered rapidly over the bar; his shoulders shook with a rhythmic beat as though he listened to gleeful driving music that no one else could hear, a groove that would not allow him to remain still.

— For a man who so strongly discourages credence to any faith, you invoke the name of the Lord a lot, do you realize this? I just wish to point out that Amanda was proactive in the feminine virtues, selfless, compassionate, look at all she did for Mather and the influence, *hmmm*, that this has had on you! Now if we could somehow *systematize* this process, that would be key – see how you've grown from your indifference and sense of victimless crimes to the caretaking of a sweet simple soul – if we could *bottle* that, as it were, and sell the stuff society-wide, we could have, that would be, the *fulcrum* the *anchor* the *hub* –

— I am still as indifferent as ever, Romeo insisted.

But Haycraft was no longer listening to him. He was off and running, with Romeo as beneficiary. Haycraft leaped into his sweeping vision of the entire city transformed in a way that, to him, would eventually (possibly) influence all of Western Civilization. He announced that he would not be able to accept the mantle of elected leadership as it would undermine his necessary independence of mind, but perhaps he could be of some use as a first-tier consultant. He alluded to the joys of boy love and omni-sexuality as a way to expand one's generous compassion. He spoke of integrity and trust, of honesty and sincerity, of guiding untarnished innocence. Of the fellowship resounding from the statue of his prophetic father bronzed forgotten in Frederick Park. In such moments Haycraft surged with boasts and confidence even as a pitiable fear came to cringe at the rims of his eyes, as though a small part of him was begging the listener to stop his tongue (stop his mind) before he went too far. A very small part of him that could not get out. Suddenly he was buying drinks for everyone, for Beau, for Glenda, even sherry for Mather who had not yet finished his shift, and who preferred brandy anyway. Declaring his creed all the while: that people should care for one another – that people *do not care enough* – that each person should strive to be excellent, excellent in the way Nietzsche described it, fine-souled, and not confined by the inadequacies of personality. He chided Romeo for his failure with Amanda, the word *failure* setting Romeo straight again on his bar stool.

— Perhaps you didn't trust in her enough, Hay suggested. You are such a bright man, Romeo, yet I recall so many evenings here when I caught the green glint in your eye, yes? and not of envy, although envy does have its hand in the pocket of jealousy's coat.... An idea for an essay, that one there. Where's my boy? I should buy a voice recorder.

— She was a narcissistic, domineering bitch, Hay, Romeo finally managed to interject.

— That is just your anger talking. Which is good, very healthy for a broken heart. Yes you loved her, Romeo, you loved her and had no idea what to do with that, you may have even forced her to break your heart somehow....

— I am not brokenhearted! cried Romeo.

With a great heaving sigh, a rise-and-fall smack of his hands against the bar, Romeo pleaded with Hay to let it lie. He tried to enjoin Beau into some other kind of conversation, asking him for his thoughts, tell him his thoughts *on anything for christ's sake.* But Haycraft could not leave him nor the subject alone. No matter what topic came up next, spurred by the hovering television – recent trades in baseball, the proposed city-county merger, a new bridge over the Ohio, a politician in Europe shellacked by hurled pies – all came back to Haycraft's belief that Romeo was not nurturing enough, that his break with Amanda was implicitly tied with his lack of faith in Trust and his antagonism to vulnerability. Haycraft's method of argument was to compare and contrast, so that the weaknesses in the bond between Romeo and Amanda were held to light against the strengths between Haycraft and his Lamb, in the context that Romeo and Amanda were past, Hay and Lamb the present, directed toward the future. As something of a new paradigm. A comparison that made Romeo bristle visibly with each further mention of *integrity* and *honesty* and *respect.*

— You think of women as compassionate and loving, Hay, but in fact they are as cunning and warlike as cats. I am not the first person to make this observation, in fact I am quoting! Amanda was, she *is* a slut, for chrissakes, she'd blow you right here if she needed twenty dollars.

— Oh, I think that's going too far. But she was giving, that Amanda.

— Giving?! She was demoralizing. *By nature.* It's what I liked about her.

Certain conversations involve little more than rebuttal and insult, yet never rise above the veneer of good-natured joking, as though the spirits of the participants swirl invisibly around them, slapping and scratching one another unseen, while their physical bodies discuss little more than weather. Quickly the dialogue between Haycraft and Romeo evolved to this level. Throughout it all Romeo appeared to become more comfortable, warming to the game of opinion, an old slyness not seen for several weeks creeping into his composure, the old arrogance and contempt twitching in his cheeks, while Haycraft hymned praises of love and cooperation and emotional generosity.

Excellent points, Romeo was honest enough to admit.

— But do you know what your problem is, Hay? You see only what you choose to see.

— I don't understand what you mean. I see *what is there.* I see what is not there, too, and wish for what is missing to arrive. Perhaps you wish to digress into a debate on perspectivism?

— Allow me an example then, Mr. Keebler, said Romeo.

Finally he indicated the curious envelope at his side, that envelope that everybody made such a point not to mention, so covered in scrawls from every angle as to resemble one of Mather Williams' creations, or as if it had been somehow woven from ink. He tapped it with two fingers, twice. For an instant he appeared to consider his next move, forming that irritable smile of his that was not really a true smile but an inward curling of the corners in his mouth, nautilus shells inscribed in his cheeks. Any reservations he may have been entertaining were discounted then. He grasped the envelope, lightly. In a performance of deliberate, operatic gestures, he folded back the metal clasp; opened the mouth. He moved carefully so as not to disturb the object from where it lay between them at the bar, going at its opening as though each small task were a separate stage that required its own clarity and presentation. As though to invite Haycraft to stop him at any given point.

Haycraft watched.

Romeo tugged the coffee-dark glossy edge of materials inside so that they peeked from the lip. He paused again, an inscrutable gleam to his eye.

— Now here is something for you, Hay, since we're just friends helping one another out, he said, tapping the packet once with his two fingers again, always the middle and ring finger together, the index and little finger flexed outward as horns.

— Here is what I'm dealing with, something I can't help seeing even when I don't want to. Allow a guy to grant you some instruction in reality.

Haycraft smiled broadly, curious. A line of unwiped ale foam formed a curved reef on his mustache. He was still humming, though gently now. Quickly he lifted his glasses to wipe his eyes. He licked the foam from his lip and went at the envelope, pulling out a number of large contact sheets. Romeo helped him, repositioning the sheets so that they were no longer upside-down. He spoke with hushed consternation:

— I've had these some two months now, and for the life of me I just don't know what to do with them. I could put them on the Web site, I guess, and make some money, get a few members back for a month or two. That's what your Amanda wants. Yet it seems, I don't know, maybe it's that I know these people, it just feels so *demeaning* to all involved. Oh, and it involves a minor, too, so that's a fact to sweat about, you can't put too fine a point on that. Getting him to sign a waiver wouldn't help at all. See that's Amanda there. She's having some fun, isn't she? You're right, Hay, she can be very giving, very selfless. As I and any number of men and women truly know. And then this page here – wait, no, look at this one, the lighting is better – that one there … the minor I'm worried about.

Romeo turned, and, setting one hand gently on Haycraft's stilled and heavy arm, called out:

— Lambret! Hey Lambret come on over, we got your star turn here.

Beau Stiles arrived at the same time as the boy. Even Glenda wandered over, swooping through the saloon doors from the kitchen to see about the fuss. Helpfully Romeo passed around the contact sheets for each to inspect. Wink McCormack, Tyrone Jeffers, the whole botched crew.

— What're you up to, Díaz? Beau asked, eyes zooming wide as he pulled the rows of photos from their thin plastic cover. Then: God *damn,* he breathed.

— Lamb? Haycraft asked.

Glenda scanned the sheet in hand and cried out singly: *Oh!* In the time it took to interpret the rows of images there she was already flinging it back down on the bar with contemptuous finality. She pushed it away, one corner rising off the tiles with the force of it and flexing with a dull *thwap* that punctuated the held-breath silence.

Haycraft did not appear to notice her disgust. He set down one sheet and picked up another, deep in study, head tilted forward to peer over his glasses. Sweat shined on his forehead, matted his hair.

— Lambret? he asked again.

Romeo sipped his scotch, his body positioned in a way that made him appear to be ducking, his lips pressed together theatrically as if he feared he might spew his liquor from laughter. Lambret stood between them, a step behind.

— Why are you looking at these, he asked, his tone more of a statement than question. Why do you have these out?

Glenda turned away from the group of men and retreated to the opposite end of the bar, to the beer taps. She snapped up the remote control and turned up the TV so that the voices there washed over the rest; she began to shift the kegs around on the floor, sending out loud, rocking shrieks of noise.

— Why are you in these pictures, Lambret? Haycraft asked. What are you doing there? When did this happen, I thought she was out west somewhere...?

— What do you mean, what am I doing there? Anantha asked me to be there.

The loose flesh on Haycraft's face lengthened; it pinched at the mouth and chin as he examined another set of sheets, holding them up to the light above.

— You didn't do this for money, certainly. Any time you have asked me for money I have given it to you.

— It was for money. It was something to do, and for money, countered Lambret.

He shrugged, slipped his hands into the back pockets of his wear-worn jeans.

— Something to do, Haycraft echoed.

— What do you think it is I do for money, H?

Under the damp fabric of his blanket-wide shirt Haycraft's back began to hump outward, a familiar and unfortunate sign. That massing of buffalo flesh in his back meant he was in difficulty. His features mixed a number of expressions, from disappointment to sadness to confusion, a perilous line of anger flattening his mouth; hot and paling radiant waves appeared over his face. He was looking for a proper reaction, certainly; after the boy's disappearance, after the running from Sutherland and the other officers, the obvious signs of continued inhalants abuse and now this, Haycraft knew he would have to say something. Yet loyalty was perhaps the strongest virtue in his soul, and the boy was an ally, both lover and mentee; there were alliances to consider. No matter what Lambret had done Hay felt the need to act compassionately, with understanding, with gentle correction. But how to do so when he felt betrayed, repulsed? When he was nearly gone on his own manic run, and not in absolute control? Throughout their time together he believed he was helping the boy with the same fervor with which he hoped to help everyone, yet Lambret's life was clearly spiralling downward and further down. An impasse, his certainties at a standoff with reality.

Surrounded by his peers, those people who, in their own way, took care of him, of Hay.

He gazed at the cruel way the boy bunched Amanda's hair in one hand; the eerie glee with which she greeted it. Where did this come from, these leers? He had never seen anything of the like in his Lamb before; he would never have agreed if someone had suggested his gentle boy was capable of the same aggressions and disrespect as any other man. As though he did not recognize the value of the person before him; as though he recognized no value in his own young life.

Having examined the entire sheaf of contacts, he returned them with care to their protective mylar wraps. He ordered them neatly, and set the short stack on top of the envelope again before pushing the pile away. Sitting quietly, Haycraft gazed at the tiled bar before him.

— Disgusting.

— You know what I do, Lambret said. You've always known, I've never hidden anything.

— Yes but I've never been forced to see, Haycraft answered. You have always been the victim in my eyes. You have always needed saving from the men in Frederick Park.

— What's the difference?

— There's a canyon of difference between violence and disgrace and shame, between all those things and acts of love. In these photos you are not being acted upon.... I do not say I don't know but I have never been forced *to look* –

— What's the difference? Lambret shouted.

— I cannot articulate the difference just now, not at this very minute, just let me *think* –

— What's the difference with what you try to do with me?

The two faced one another, Haycraft on his stool, the boy standing yet still smaller than his companion. In the pause that grew there Hay took deep rapid breaths, working his hands over his knees; his humming swerved over discordant melodies. They stared at one another for a time, for a long time, through a silence that beat away the light music of the stereo serenade, the commercials on the TV. No one in the room – even in the scattering of patrons sitting at their tables – spoke a word. At the end of it Haycraft stopped looking at the boy, inclining his head so that his eyes met some vague place on the floor, and saying, almost as to himself:

— I will not enter into this discussion in a public place. Not here. There is a difference between the public and the private, boy! I have no idea what to say just now, anyway. I don't....

The door of the Theatre Room scraped open, Mather Williams whistling as he came to the top of the stairs with his broom. He swept the first stair with concentration, then stopped, his attention drawn to one of the fans stirring above the tables below. His whistling ceased.

Tyrone Jeffers leaned forward over the bar and called down to Romeo.

— Where is she off to, anyway? She gonna come back and dance for us at the Primrose soon?

— This is not about her! Haycraft shouted.

Glenda peered up from where she fiddled with keg valves, telling Hay to quiet down. The order had the same impact on him as if he were ten again and a neighbor's mother had turned on him with passionate correction. The sight of this seemed to embolden Glenda, and she stood quickly to focus her attention on the group of them.

— And you, Romeo, get those pictures out of sights. You ought to be ashamed, trying to embarrass your friends like that, I would've thought you a better man. Every one of you, I'll stand you a drink right now if you all go about your business like this never happened.

— Oh, this happened all right, said Haycraft.

He could not look at the boy; he kept his face lowered toward the tiles. His back had arched to its full extent, a thick mass of bulk appearing to slide up ready to overtake his neck, swallow his head. When Lambret reached to touch his shoulder, Haycraft shrugged him away. He reached for his pint but his shaking hands knocked over the glass. Beer spilled in a wide carbonated skirt over the bar tiles, covering the manila folder, foaming then subsiding, staining rows of contact sheets and ruining with great splatches of liquored ink Romeo's notes for Amanda.

— Beau I'm terribly sorry, Haycraft nearly hollered.

— No sweat, I'll get you another.

The television whispered over the hiss of press-poured beer. When the glass arrived Haycraft gulped it down in three long pulls, throat popping with each hard swallow, the red welts on his skin flaring in the bar light. He ordered another, fingers hammering the envelope as he refused to look at anyone, his face gone near to maroon, anxiety pulsing about him, forehead a geyser of wetness. Romeo's satirical grin had fallen from his own face; he stared at Hay with mouth agape.

— I don't understand what difference any of this makes, Lambret said, quietly but insistently, from behind them all.

— Hush. I do not wish to speak to you any longer.

The statement left no options to the boy. It was so unlike Haycraft – who left everything about his conversations and behavior open and accepting of revision – to speak with such finality. The arch tone made everyone feel scolded, lowered. Nobody looked at anyone else, except for the boy staring hard at Haycraft's thick back, at the thinning hair combed over the crown, at the foot of his glasses' arm slipping out from behind the man's crimsoned ear, at the inflamed creases that gashed across his neck. *Whatever*, the boy muttered, finally.

He turned up his eyes in teenage exasperation, shook his head violently. Believing he had saved some scrap of personal dignity with that word, he did not linger for long. He climbed the stairs toward the exit and stopped beside Mather Williams, who swayed gently with his broom, apparently saddened by his own perception of the mood at the bar. Lambret did not speak to him, but at the sight of Mather the boy turned abruptly, and hurried back to the table with its stack of books. Grabbing one without a glance, he told Haycraft he would see him around as he passed behind the row of stools (the most indirect path available), Haycraft still seated and unmoving, looking nowhere but at the golden light in his own refreshed pint, not acknowledging the boy's goodbye. Lambret did not look back, either; as a final gesture he leaped to swat the bottommost sail of the windmill outside, sending loud reverberations echoing through the entranceway and swarming the room briefly, a sound disturbing and hollow. Then the doors clicked shut behind him.

— Good luck, Haycraft said, and raised his glass in a high lonesome toast.

§

The aftermath spread over several nights, but only the last holds importance worth recounting. It arrived deep, musty, and slow; the conversations with their banalities, complaisant platitudes – the sheer idiocy of bar talk – rose and veered without harm or worry. Beau Stiles joined in to get as sloshed as the rest of them, a development Glenda could detect before anyone. Those gathered allowed Haycraft to vent and spew as he had each night since Lambret left, thinking it best not to bother him after the recent revelations and declarations. *Hmmmm*, he hummed. *Yes, well, it's all very disappointing*, he blurted out after silent self-communion, apropos of nothing. *I feel like one of those European politicians with pie on his face.* And *hmmm* he hummed again, his melodies gaining velocity between outbursts on the alleged corruption of the sheriff's office rumbling through the media at the time – *We should arrange a pie for them!* he shouted – a subject that somehow directed him to express frustration at two new massage parlors within the district, a fact that made him fear for the unfortunate women who gained employment there, especially. Perhaps he should approach these women? Primarily he would like to learn the points of view of Asian women in that industry, to glean how they perceived their supposed submissiveness. Maybe he could convince them to unionize.

— Pies in the faces of them all, sighed Haycraft. We look to the oldest of our cultures for a sign of where to go, and the best they can manage is a pie in the face. Such impotence.

— People don't got many options, opined Wink rhetorically. That's what it is, man, that's it right there.

Haycraft ignored him. Did anyone realize, he began, did anyone notice, that these new developments, sad as they were to the attentive eye, were mirrored *even in the natural world about them?* Bad tidings abounded. Haycraft had observed a directional shift in the common winds, it had come to his attention at 12:34 PM the previous Thursday as he began his rounds; slaughterhouse stink had settled over his sidewalks, an unnatural shift that reflected his uncertainty in the rising sun, which, he declared, no longer could be found directly in the East but now followed a trajectory limning the South – in case no one else had remarked upon it.

Bad signs indeed, Glenda intoned, taking Haycraft's omens as signifiers of a much different sort than he intended. She suggested that now might be a good time for him to go home and rest, a suggestion to which Haycraft agreed and yet refused, arguing that as much as he might like to leave for the safety of home he simply could not do so as yet, there were still two hours on his schedule and such further disruptions as he had suffered this past month might leave him not just forlorn but entirely incapacitated, a horrible lot to befall a man when there was still so much work to be done – and massage parlors, of all things to add to the common routes of schoolchildren! – and what would they say to him if he confessed that just the night before, as he walked home from this very place worried over the whereabouts of his Lambret, he noted the flash and wink of the midnight stars, then gazed in dumb slack-mouthed awe as he realized the moon rejoined them in similar flash and wink, a celestial bob-and-weave of syncopated (if irregular) shudders of light directed, possibly, at him – Haycraft – like some manner of sublime Morse code?

— I don't even understand Morse code! Haycraft bellowed in exasperation. Do you see the matters I must deal with?

And before any of those gathered there jumped to foregone conclusions, Haycraft continued, he wanted to disclose right then and there that he fully understood how unusual this notion of star-written messages could be, in fact, *was*, and yet there they had it, he was not capable of providing his friends with any further explanation.

— You each know that at heart I strive to be a rational man, said Hay.

There is a heaven and a star for you, Mather joined in. *I miss my star, Romeo, I miss our Miss Amanda.*

— Oh, do shut him up, Haycraft demanded.

— I can buy you another brandy, Mather, beckoned Romeo. I'm on a tear tonight, why don't you come with me.

Mather said yes he *did* want to come with him; Mather said he would like nothing more than to come with Romeo and even to drive, *You promised me a drive in your car, me driving, Romeo!* he cried. Sporting his best catch at a winning smile, Romeo nodded. The two leaned toward one another with inclined, conspiratorial heads. They brought their drinks together in warm brotherly laughter and ordered more.

In his agitated state, Haycraft identified in those two inclined heads another social wrong to be righted. He roared with fiery righteousness to quiet all before him, declaring that so much alcohol poured into a man like Mather could not be any good, and did no one consider the repercussions of psychotropic drugs on Mather's system, on such a small and skinny frame? *I tell you of bad omens written in the very elements and you people fill a medicated man with drink right before me? Do you believe I reference wind, sun, stars, for my benefit only?*

But nobody listened. No one had a response aside from hushing him up with a room-wide *shhhh*, a mirthful reaction Haycraft had long ago become accustomed to and yet against which he never had became inured. He set to working the longer corners of his mustache through his lips, clenching and unclenching them beneath the amber light of the bar, his breaths heaving in hefty bursts. But he did stay quiet.

In the end Glenda drove him home that night, telling him *A good night's rest is what you need* as she tucked him in.

— A good night's rest and tomorrow you might see things in a very different light, no matter which direction the sun comes up from.

The different light would be a darker one.

Back at the Don Quixote, Romeo was on his tear with Mather in tow, dragging his companion through drink after drink, matching him shot for shot, their arms around one another and their heads sopped together.

I miss her, Romeo, Mather said.

I miss her, too, Romeo answered.

Beau busied himself by switching between channels on the TV, testing at what directions he could point the remote and still get the TV to respond, seeing whether or not the signal would bounce off window glass or steel. Wink McCormack wanted his shot at it, too. Tyrone Jeffers made an attempt from the stairwell. They took no notice of Romeo stumbling off to the bathroom; they never saw Mather leave. Their blunted and warbling senses hardly even registered Romeo's return, or his rusty voice asking if anyone had seen his keys.

— That little fucker, Romeo said.

He raced up the stairs and into the alley where he kept his car, but it was gone. He laughed in surprised recognition, in wry disbelief, of his charge's ingenuity. He set his hands to his hips, then pulled his arms tightly around himself and began the walk home; the night was wet and creeping with cold.

THE
SUTHERLAND
VIEW

LET ME TELL YOU ONE THING UP front: I have never been good at aftermaths. Get in, get out, let everyone else talk later if they want. That's the head you got to have for this line of work. At least how I see it. You think too much, start wondering down the could-haves and should-haves, you end up hurt or worse. You are not doing your job. So I don't let much stick to me. That is not to say that I am indifferent.

The night in question. At the start I was more concerned with the hot coffee in my sock. Me and my partner Ricky Keach had just finished with a domestic between a guy and his wife at an apartment complex, one of those subsidized shoebox places. She'd been running around with a neighbor and he learned of it and had had enough, broke some things of hers ... things in the home I mean, not her bones or anything. The neighbors were out to see the commotion, and this nice old lady said she had some coffee and would I like some for me and my partner. This was pretty late, around two-thirty, three in the morning. She told me she was the one who called, she lived alone and heard stuff crashing upstairs so she called. Nice lady. *Nice lady with Parkinson's*: When she turned with my cup she lost her grip and the stuff fell right on my shoe, soaking me clean to the skin. That doesn't sound important in light of later events, but that coffee was blister hot. By the time we got into the cruiser it hurt so bad I had to take off my shoe and the sock and give my foot some air.

901T hits the radio, ambulance needed at a traffic accident. No big deal. 907K, paramedics dispatched to Frederick Park. Not the kind of thing that registers in your head when you have a burnt foot and hoots of laughter on a grass-bare lawn behind you. Keach drove while I wrung my hot sock out the window, preferring not to talk about it. But once the crowd was behind us we both started laughing, laughing on the hard luck that seems mine alone, always. I was trying to be a good sport about the whole thing – it wasn't like it was her fault she got the Parkinson's – but I'd be lying to say it didn't hurt. This stuff was hot, McDonald's-lawsuit hot, I was scalded, man.

No, I didn't tell Keach that. Some things just feel too trivial, and between guys there are methods of denying the other certain satisfactions.

We didn't follow the call immediately. We figured the driver must have been pretty drunk or stoned to crash his car in the park bad enough for an ambulance. There's only the one lane winding through the place. And I didn't want to talk about my foot so I asked Keach, How polluted you got to be to manage a crash like that? and Keach, being Keach, he brought it right back to the matter at hand, he said maybe the driver had spilled that lady's coffee on himself and that's why he needed an ambulance.... Maybe that lady's the one we need to take down around here, Keach said, she's wreaking havoc all over Old Towne with her damned coffee. Fuckin' Ha Ha.

So we were not taking it real serious – a bender in Frederick Park is just another mishap blip in every Old Towne night. We didn't think it serious till the medics radioed in for backup. They said the driver had refused aid and was threatening them. They said he had an open head wound but when they tried to help he swung a tire jack. They wouldn't try anything until the police got there, they said. And then get this: *the medic laughed.* We got us a wild one, he said, and chuckled again.

Keach roared us off with dome lights flashing. I worked with my coffee-soaked sock, my foot stinging from a pretty good burn by now.

Put your foot under the dash, Keach said, and I'll get the air blowing down there.

I did but it didn't help. It helped a little.

He said the medics would have burn ointment in the ambulance. I laughed, flexing my toes so that the air could get in there. I mean how did the coffee soak through so fast to my toes? I asked, out loud. Keach said it must have sunk through the laces.

Two cops rushing down the road in our cruiser with a wet sock flapping out the window, me wondering at what people saw as we passed, what they must have thought. Police lights flashing, flying cruiser, wet sock – your tax dollars at work, good citizens. And this was all just *so me*: Despite my best efforts I have managed little in the way of honor and dignity in this life. What makes it so hard to laugh at now, and the reason why I'm going on about it, is that it was that sock, that nice lonely old lady's coffee, what caused the whole night to go as bad as it did. I can't get past that.

Because it kept me in the car, see. That's the whole point. We pull into the park and I'm a cop with one bare foot, stinging still. It's not the worst of emergencies, and we're not even the first unit there – Ferguson and Magers already stood with their lights on the scene – but it was enough to make me feel ridiculous when Keach pulls up and gets out to join them, leaving me alone. The streetlight was out on this stretch of the park road, our only light came from the ambulance and the two cruisers; the headlights on the wrecked BMW were still on, too, glowing out into the groves of trees, playing shadows in the dark where the park-freaks hid. The Beamer had run up over the curb and flattened two tires, hit one of the park benches in front of the old mayor's statue, and rested with its fender up on the bench seat. Ferguson and Magers stood talking to a man crouched holding a tire iron. Black male about thirty-five to forty, five-foot-five maybe one hundred twenty pounds, greasy gray undershirt and black pants.

I don't know everything that was said at first. Keach crossed the front of our cruiser asking what's up as a paramedic approached, a real looker, too, very small with short blonde hair that looked natural, I'd never seen her around before and of course speaking of honor and dignity here I am working a wet sock over my foot in a hurry, which is not a simple task. A sock that's tight in the first place, dry. She repeated what we'd heard on the radio, said this guy had a bad gash on his head but when they tried to help him he got angry and lashed out with the tire iron.

We haven't done anything since, she said, he swung at us so we called you all.

Good girl, Keach said. Keach has a way about him that allows him to say things like that without having to answer for it. If I said the same thing in the exact same tone of voice I'd end up with a complaint on my score sheet. That is a difference between Keach and me for which I will always envy and hate him.

For example. They walked toward the scene together and Keach laughed at something she said – just a short sharp laugh – and I figured he must have been explaining why I had not yet gotten out of the car. That bothered me. Keach is already married and has a kid and he says he loves his wife but me, I'm still looking, I'm open to meeting somebody nice, a nice girl who understands what a cop's life is like and doesn't fault him for it. Like an EMT, for example. Keach knows this but it does not occur to him at opportune times. That grates at me since he is my partner and of all people we are supposed to have one another's back and all that, at all times, the fraternity, all that. Instead, at opportune times he likes to bring up the fact of my inhaler, or the steroids they got me on for breathing right. Last I see of him his hand is placed gently on her shoulder, petting it like everything will be okay. This touched a sore nerve. We have discussed this very sort of thing before, how easygoing he is with women and me being, well, not so easygoing. He's supposed to help me out and not be my competition. I made a mental note to discuss this again with him afterward.

The sock. Maybe I was a little agitated and rushed feeling. The simple task of returning the sock to my foot was not working out well. And you get pretty jacked up in these situations, you don't know what you're getting into, if the guy is a pussy or some jackoff PCP fiend who needs shattered bones to take him in. So your adrenaline gets pumping and maybe that's why I was having such trouble with the damn sock. I had it by the mouth half up my foot and was trying to slip on the rest to where the toes go in and then shimmy the thing up from there. But that coffee had burned me pretty good and the sock was still warm and damp and the thing just *stung*, man, it did not want to go on. There's yelling outside and I look up and Ferguson's stance has changed, he has his hand on his stick and his left arm out before him. I couldn't hear what he said, there was chatter on the radio but he had his hand out like he was telling the guy to take it easy.

We're worried about that cut you have there, how did you hurt yourself? Keach asked.

And the guy just screams. No words, just: AAAAAHHH!

That stumps the whole gang right there. That just shuts up everybody. What do you say to that? AAAAAHHH! He screams it over and over. The three cops pause, then Magers – who didn't have a stick, he's a detective – steps up. The guy swings the tire iron at him, shouts *Back off I can fix it, I can fix it fine myself.* Which only serves to make the officers haw-haw a little. Which may have been wrong, cause it upset the guy. He started screaming louder AAAHHH and *Stay away from me, I got it under control here,* stuff like that.

I'm in trouble, leave me alone, he says.

Magers asks him what kind of trouble.

Bad trouble, man, this ain't my car.

Whose car is it? Magers asks.

Nothing, no response.

Where'd you get the car? asks Keach.

Nothing. Then: *My head hurts.*

Well why don't you let us help you with your head? asks Magers. He has his flashlight up and the guy's face is covered with blood, I can see that from the car. Maybe that's why I didn't recognize him. Nighttime, lights flashing, his face streaked all over with blood – you wouldn't recognize your own mother.

So we had the lights, the blood, a wrecked car, the tire iron. And I had my issues with the foot, the sock. I'm wheezing too but that's not unusual. Still it's an uneasy situation. Our perp starts moving around, kind of hopping while he stays in this weird crouch, and times like that you pay more attention to a guy's moves than to his face. I yanked off the sock and decided to do without, just go with the shoe.

Keach had moved around to the other side of the car, trying to keep the guy from seeing all three cops at once. So the guy keeps hopping around, trying to keep track of them all. They tell him to let go of the jack, just put it down, stay calm, the usual. He gives them that scream again.

AAAAHHH!

Then he starts shouting every nonsense you couldn't think of unless you had the same head. It only adds to the tension.

Finally he does let go of the jack, I don't know if he dropped it from being so worked up or if he meant to let go, but at the sound of that metal clanging on the pavement the officers were on him. And my shoe is tight and I think my foot has swollen from the burn, but with the ruckus outside I'm needed so I push my foot in no matter the hurt and don't even bother with the laces, I'm already out the door and hobbling over fast.

Because it's a melee now and things are all weird: Keach gave him pepper spray and the guy did not go down. He cries out and covers his eyes, but with his other hand he gets hold of Keach's wrist. He's kicking shins. You do not see that kind of reaction to pepper spray very often, especially from a perp this small, and I don't know what anybody could be thinking to grab a cop's arm like that. Here is a bit of sound advice: You just do not do that to an officer. You do not make a move on him. Especially in the presence of other officers. Magers had his flashlight and Ferguson his nightstick, and they went at it and they did their jobs right. That's when I came up with one squishing shoe and a limp. I wanted to help but wasn't sure what to do, exactly. Three on one already, I couldn't see where to get in. All I could see was the mistake.

They didn't have him on the ground, see; he was up against the car. A little wiry guy, stronger than he looked and thrashing hard for sweet life. He got in a good pop with his elbow into Magers' throat, I saw that clearly in my flashlight. The blow forced Magers to step back, and through that little opening where their two bodies parted, what I saw in my flashlight changed the entire situation, it just recast the whole night. Cause that's when I realized I *knew* this perp. I knew he was nuts but mostly harmless. I knew something must be badly wrong for all of us to be here in this situation at this time of morning. But

I didn't say anything, I couldn't, it was a full-out fight. And at this point I wasn't thinking *I have to save Mather Williams from this grave misunderstanding.*

If I'd shouted his name it would not have made any difference. He was screaming. Mather had some big lungs in that scrawny body of his. They had him backed up against the car and that's the only reason I can think of that kept him standing, because the boys had thumped him pretty good. Grunts and swears and everybody pissed off, and Ferguson kept trying to get Mather's arm pulled behind his back, but somehow Mather kept twisting it right back out. It felt like I stood a long time there watching, not sure what to do exactly – not shouting Mather's name, which I don't think would have changed anything, but still.

Yeah it was a real fight. You get in close on a fighter and things are going to get handled. You're hitting and not paying attention to where your hands go. And Mather's hand got hold of Keach's gun. He got a grip on it in his holster. Now that one paramedic, the pretty one, she said she thought Mather was trying to grab hold of something to stay up on his feet, and in the scuffle that happened to be Keach's gun. Which makes sense and may even be true. But I don't think that matters. I say: There are a few things you just do not do with police officers. A cop does not have time to think "he's grabbing my gun only to stay up on his feet." He's thinking only of his weapon being grabbed. That is a grave danger to which we are prepared to respond. Mather grabbed the butt of the gun and pulled, he pulled hard enough that Keach wheeled off balance, his belt winched up one side. Keach yelled out, "He's trying my gun," and *my gun my gun my gun!* That's all a cop needs to hear.

We performed exactly as trained: We met the assailant with enough force to prevent any further threat to ourselves. We all pulled trigger together, every one of us but Keach that is, who was doing his best to get out of the way.

Eighteen rounds from three automatics go quick. Fifteen shots hit. Only the last one was fatal, as I understand it. Most hit his legs and arms and the car. Or else missed outright. And Mather, he didn't say anything, he just let out this big cough of breath like he wanted to clear his throat but couldn't. He stiffened up on his feet, pinched his face like he suddenly felt an awful shiver or stepped on a live wire and got the big shock. He raised his hands about halfway up his body, the way you imagine sleepwalkers, and fell back a step, banged up against the passenger side of the car. Then down to the ground. And that was it, man. Game over.

§

It has taken me a lot of time and I cannot say I fully understand the events of that night, but I do feel okay about them. It has cost me a certain standing among certain circles, as everybody knows. There is the whole "magic bullet" thing with my gun, which everybody knows about thanks to the newspapers. Every round was accounted for during the investigation except a couple of mine. They never did find either one of them even though they practically dug up a new park looking. Williams had one wound that didn't have a bullet still in it, through the bicep of his right arm. I like to think that one may have been mine. That one was mine and the other one missed altogether. I like to think then that I did not kill Mather.

Not that I'm saying people should fault the other guys. We each did exactly what we had been taught to do, and anyone else in our shoes would have done the same thing. It's a bitch to get other people to understand that, to see it. No one wants to believe you.

Usually I don't think much about work. People are ugly and do awful things and I see it every day and all the acts mix together in your head. You convince yourself that the implications are not worth pursuing. Sometimes they come up anyway. But this night is the only one I think of on my own, playing it again over and over. It's the only time I've been involved in a man's death, and it doesn't even matter that I knew Mather, some things you just do not forget.

You wish you could have done things differently, that life would have turned out in a different way. It sounds ridiculous, but I am being completely honest when I say that I blame the sock. A hard thing to get your head around: If me and Keach had not answered that call at the house; if the old woman hadn't been kind and just wanted to be left alone, she would not have offered us the coffee; if she hadn't had Parkinson's, Mather Williams might still be alive. It is exactly this kind of thinking that keeps me from reflecting on my job very often. Because there's nothing you can do. An old woman drops coffee on your shoe and it doesn't seem possible that this will lead directly to a man getting shot. It's like you are powerless to change anything, like life is going to play out any kind of way it wants. You want to feel like you have a direct influence on what happens to you and on what you cause to happen to others, but I wonder if we have much say in it at all.

My conscience is clean.

A
HEART
IN THE
HEART
OF THE
CITY

THE NEXT ANYONE SAW OF HAYCRAFT
Keebler would be in the afternoon light of Mather's wake. He
looked strange to the regulars; they were used to seeing him in
the clouded glow of bar light, the shimmering halos of streetlights, the pale touch of moonlight – the man always crowded
by darkness. Following Mather's death Hay had stopped coming
to the bar, and again it had been Glenda who sought him out,
using the Stiles' pickup truck to ferry him to the wake held at
the Don Q.

Not only did he appear different to them, Haycraft *had*
changed; they all remarked upon it, among themselves. They
were all angry and disappointed with Romeo, too – he had gone
too far, they said; that fiasco with the photographs wasn't funny,
and what had he been up to with Mather that night, leaving the
man alone to his own designs, his blood all polluted? So Romeo
got hurt by Anantha's leaving, that didn't give him rights to
take the rest of the regulars down with him, to destroy their

haven. Wink McCormack and Johnny Reb would not even sit by Díaz at the bar anymore.

The bare rooms, heavy with loss and the guilt of failing one of their own, with the sense of communal waste, turned yet more grave with the weight of Haycraft's distress – Lambret had not come. No one could find him, he had disappeared again. To look at Hay was to see a man shrunk into impenetrable misery.

He spoke of a heart and mind filled with soot. He was having obvious difficulty staying awake. Haycraft sat immobile, unanimated, at one with his bar stool. The single gesture that kept him from appearing catatonic – aside from the cyclic imbibing of pints, but that was movement that did not register in this crowd – lay in his use of a rusty roof nail found in the alley: Resolutely Hay tapped the sharp point against his open palm. The gesture worried Glenda terribly.

Such a forlorn sight even penetrated the dense indifference of Romeo Díaz (much more so now that McCormack and Reb had absconded to the other end of the bar); he had only intended a little provocation, he said in his own defense. But his little provocations – even he understood – bore a great deal of responsibility for Mather's death, and for Anantha's (his Amanda) abandonment of him, and he was beginning to question his own motives in everything. He told Beau:

— I only meant a bit of mischief, man. To take a little hot wind out of Hay's sails. No illusions, right? He was going on about the purity of his boy, the two of them holding hands making a mockery of everything I stand for, which I can appreciate in theory, but I'm sitting on these photos, you know? You think I was happy to see the kid with this woman I considered to be my own wife?

Beau shrugged, sighed, showed his haggard, put-upon face. He wasn't up to this kind of talk; he *believed* in wakes, and was there to think upon Mather Williams.

— It's temporary, this thing with Hay, Beau said.

Beau tried to believe his patrons' lives were not his business.

Despite his avowal to care for Hay, he could do only so much. Haycraft was an adult, after all. But he did not appreciate what Romeo had done – with Mather, with Haycraft, with Anantha and the boy – even if he quietly believed it best that Lamb had left to seek his own pursuits. Glenda agreed; they did not speak about such things at the bar.

After the wake, Haycraft relapsed into his avoidance of the club. *The Old Towne Fair Dealer* was no longer left skidding across the sidewalk, or waving beneath windshield wipers. And no one from the bar saw him at all, even when Tyrone Jeffers attempted to meet him on the old schedule. Haycraft skipped the funeral; he missed cashing a check from the state. Weeks later Chesley Sutherland informed Beau and Glenda that he had glimpsed a man he took to be Haycraft – he'd seen suspenders and piped trousers, although admittedly he had not had time to note the telling details of sandals or shoes – gesticulating from the rails of an overpass at the cars passing under, holding by the nape of its neck a small, helpless dog. Information that frightened Glenda enough that she went in search of Haycraft in his apartment. But all she found there was a dirty room rank with a weedlike odor, a sink stacked with unwashed dishes, empty cans of acrylic gold spray paint and thinner spoiled on crusty rags, the floor crunching underfoot on the rinds of dry toenail clippings. His notebooks lay in tatters, some ripped from their spiral coils and drawn asunder, others bent and flayed as though their attacker had not had the strength to destroy them. On one page bared to the air she spotted the line *he who never strays has gone astray*, naked and alone on the bleached paper, striking in the light of an ascending white moon.

§

It all wore Glenda down especially. Despite that Mather had been living in Romeo's Ruin for over a year, she still considered herself his legitimate protector, similar to her distant watching-over of Keebler, who she had believed was more adept at caring for himself than Mather was. To her mind, Romeo was just helping an old girl out.

Glenda attracted the inconsequential by habit, as though her heart could not resist exposing itself to those most likely to harm it. In the crowded street, the cramped bus, in her own club – the damaged mind drew to Glenda's face.

Riding the bus to the grocery a young woman approached her with the words *Mother, where have you been? I've been searching for you everywhere.*

— What do you mean, I'm not your mother, Glenda replied.

— I've been waiting for you such a long time, Mother, the woman answered. It's not kind of you to leave me, your only daughter, alone like that for so long.

She felt the stares of the surrounding strangers.

— I don't know who you are. Get away from me, this is my stop, she said, bolting down the aisle at the first hiss of hydraulic doors.

Fifteen different passengers the girl could have chosen, yet she singled out Glenda. This was her life. Glenda met such advances nowadays with her best meager defenses, yet still, whenever she saw that young woman again, she could not help but offer her some small gift: a stick of gum, a pastry baked in the Don Q kitchen, simple conversation. And then that person, often without even a name to attach to them, would enter the universe of her constant worries.

— I'm getting too old and frankly these people bug hell out of me now, she confessed to Romeo. I just don't have the patience anymore, there are too many of you out there.

Empathy showed itself early in her life. As a child she was sent out by her mother to the homes of the senile to dish food and a young face they could talk to for a while. On Sundays she accompanied her preacher to serve communion to those too ill or old or both to get themselves to church. At the time she believed such care and giving behavior made a difference, and that was what it was all about. She performed her duties earnestly.

My barefoot days she called them, running about Sassafras in a knee-length poplin dress, pedaling her bike an hour's ride to Black Mountain (*the highest point in the state,* her father often pointed out to her, proud). She would hike up the nether trail to her favorite butte overlooking the life-scale topographical map, the display of town and farms as far as she could fathom.

There on the butte, with her callused heels stoppered against a limestone shelf, arms hugging her knees to her soft round chin, Glenda Cottle reached a simple conclusion about the world: People were too stingy with their love and care for one another.

And even as a young girl, she understood that despite a strong loyalty to her family and to the mountains circling her town, she would one day leave them all. The city was the place for her.

A voice scholarship brought her to Montreux's university; she came armed only with a single cardboard suitcase and a battered Slingerland guitar. It was just after the Korean War and Montreux was thriving with its small airport that housed the 101st Airborne Division, the economy still tingling from the drive of war. Coffeehouses and bars kept the servicemen busy on furloughs – *where I got my* real *education,* Glenda liked to say. She sang to the boys three nights a week for extra money, sitting on a wooden stool and strumming the five or six chords she knew while reciting the tales of John Henry, the Fox and the Goose, songs about love and bootlegging. The men scamped for her; she had been quite the beauty back then: waist-length sable hair, dark green eyes, a sturdy but curvaceous frame. And she had her voice, too, a strong mezzosoprano she could tremelo with precise control.

Beau said he fell in love with her because of that voice, but Glenda didn't come barefoot from Sassafras quite *that* naïve. She had been something else to look at – and she knew what she was doing with the length of her skirts worn slightly hiked up the thigh when she played, her legs crossed demurely to situate the guitar. She chose Beau over the others because of his sweetness. Because of his sweetness and because it seemed a good fit. Sometimes he backed her on the upright bass, grooving in his drab Army uniform, small but broad-shouldered, his face young and smile-lined, eyes as blue as cornflowers, hair blond and already thinning at the temples. He'd seen combat in Korea but seemed unaffected by it, aside from a valentine heart tattoo with its pledge to an unfamiliar woman's name. He didn't seem affected by anything but boyish joy, his laughter springing quickly, engaging everyone; he was exactly what she wanted.

Which was not to become her mother. Her father had been a charmer who could spout moral politic on command, and she revered him (although as she matured and better understood him, the affection sprang more from amusement than adoration); she remembered her mother as a dour and sarcastic nag. Her mother's spoken thoughts claimed laundry and dinner and the duties of children. Most of all she spoke of money; that, and the bitterness of constant giving in to the whims of her husband. When not making shrewd comment on the family's financial matters (*your father spends more paying off officials than he charges for whisky!*), she was wondering aloud if the sheriff's new baby was truly his own, or where a local insurance salesman had come up with a hundred dollars to drop into the church collection plate. The private lives of postal workers, lowly clerks, and especially their wives, were of prime importance to her. Particularly the question of how anyone could afford anything.

Glenda took her father's stories of the woman's beauty in youth as personally interpreted history. The woman Glenda knew was small and stout, paunchy at the arms and face, the mouth a tight line with seismic, vertical furrows stretching above and below. Her mother's eyes were oddly clear, but the flesh around them was mottled and wasted. Her voice – shrill and wracked – a constant termagant's yammer. No, none of that was for Glenda: the babies at sixteen, speculation and comment on everybody else's business, the passionate drive for cash in hand above all else. A little fun first, thank you.

She was nineteen when she married Beau. She knew she wanted a family – a large one – and that she liked artists and liked also to help as many people as possible to have a good time. That was big for her; to get others to let loose. As a result, several clubs would follow that bore the stamp of the family Stiles: Beau's Place, their first; The Rascal Scrap – which she didn't enjoy as much as it was a straight-up dramshop with no kitchen for her to practice her creative gifts, cooking soon overtaking song as her art of choice; and then her favorite, The Storefront Assembly, which served as an experimental groundwork for the Don Quixote, with gospel musicals composed by many of the patrons themselves as a highlight. The place thrived a good ten years until Glenda decided to ban smoking from the premises. She was pregnant with their son Damon then, and the Assembly's gradual demise barely touched her.

— But you run a club, it's like catching a bug, Glenda would explain. Once it's gone you begin to feel this odd itch, wondering where all the people in your life went.

Pass another twelve years with Beau directing highway construction, and then the *Come Back to Montreux!* campaign began and gave rise to the notion of the Quixote. The first twenty years of their marriage had passed in Old Towne; until the mid-seventies when the troubles began, they'd had nothing but happy memories there. Beau and Glenda were willing to stake their efforts in the revitalization of what they believed to be the most precious district in the city – the heart of the populace.

Glenda was proud of their accomplishment even if the club, the community, the city had not met the level of success they had envisioned. She complained often about how worn out she felt each day. Her Damon was grown and away; her hands – rounded as puff pastry with the same fate that saddled her body and sagged her face – ached and burned with the exhaustion of bread-baking, the slicing of vegetables and meats, the lift and heft of commercial-sized containers of condiments, jeroboams of wine. Mothering over Mather Williams the while, one of those lost souls who picked her face off the street, but one whom she did not have the heart to push away.

Now she nagged Beau to keep a more forthright hand on the accounting; she speculated to Damon over the phone and in letters of her suspicions of certain lesbian affairs begun in her club – and was astonished to hear her son comment that she sounded like she did not approve. *It's not that I don't approve,* she countered, *my approval doesn't even come into the matter....* And yet she could not come up with any better word for what she was after.

Then there was the clouded case of Haycraft Keebler. Like Beau, she had known his father, and had known Hay as a boy of capricious imagination and startling, precocious intelligence; and, alongside Beau, she had watched and learned that vote-buying wasn't as accepted a practice in Montreux as it had been in Sassafras, and saw the boy manifest himself into a portrait of a distraught psyche who took to sleeping in meadows. There was also his innocently voiced confusion over his sexuality, and then the long hospital stay after a male prostitute beat him badly back in Reagan's first term. The surprise introduction of Lambret Dellinger and her disdain for Beau's suggestion that they hire the boy to get him off the street performing God-knew-what for money – Glenda let everyone and anyone in hearing distance understand how she felt about it all. She did not know why. She suspected perhaps Hay was trying to balance something in his life by his companionship with the boy, to correct his experience with the hustler who beat him as a youth.

Not that she was interested in psychoanalyzing someone else's motivations.

Burying Mather, Glenda felt caught in a permanent mood of

disappointment and loss. She had wanted a large family but they had managed only Damon. Which may have been for the best, as their son appeared well-adjusted to the confines of adulthood. Their other efforts – taking Haycraft under wing, then Mather – had not been as successful. Look at how their lives had turned out: one man dead, the other disappeared, with stories seeping to the Don Q of sightings and clues that only worried her further: a bulky man in an ill-fitted dress watching children at a play-ground; gold graffiti messages spotted on overpasses, telephone boxes, alleyway pavements: *has the lamb lain down?* And *i seek my king unanointed*; also the simple *i love you i miss you l.* Enough to fan her worries to panic. But none of her visits to Haycraft's apart-ment found him there. He had become a voice heard outside a window, a reference in someone else's outrageous conversation, a face on a bus already passing her by.

So she trudged to the Don Quixote kitchen every morning as she had every day for over ten years, hoping this period of time and its mood would pass over. As it had before. But then *she didn't feel up to it.* How many times had she worked alongside Beau mopping up some mess in the kitchen, mixing spices and sauces, garlic or paprika heavy in her nostrils and tasted on her tongue, swimming in her sweat?

She felt much older than her sixty-two years. Her head hurt constantly. She had taken to wearing smocks. Before Haycraft disappeared, she was bumming Lithium off him to keep herself level and calm, her perpetual exhaustion throwing her at the gates of hysteria on a nightly basis. And for no reason, no reason at all that she could identify.

All she remembered of the past decade were the residual effects of uncompromising effort. Fatigue. And then to see hapless Mather, a man she considered as unfortunate as any, to die like that. *And do you mean to tell me Chesley Sutherland, after all we've done for him, couldn't have stopped this from happening?* she asked Beau, she asked Romeo, she asked anyone. These thoughts –

moreover, this lingering mood – led her to investigate the possibility of change. She'd founded the place and named it the Don
Q as a metaphor for one's ability to create reality. It occurred to
her she'd spent her life fostering others' versions of so-called
reality, and she decided these other versions, the ones she saw
day to day and night to night, were sad.

Beau was already receiving the little Social Security he was
due and she would begin to draw from that also, and soon. They
had a smattering of catering business that, with a touch more
effort, some advertising maybe and a little legwork on Beau's
part, could easily reach a sustainable point. Thus not long after
Mather's wake, with investigations by civil groups and the police
into his whereabouts before the shooting and the amount of
alcohol he was served at her bar adding to the pressures of
simply keeping the Don Q doors open, Glenda announced to
the regulars that she had never signed on to be the caretaker
of lost souls. She said her lifetime of kindness had been like an
investment with no return, and she was sick of it. It was time
to shut the place down and move on.

§

The announcement met with little resistance and surprising
fanfare. Montreux ignored the place nightly, but over a career of
fourteen years the Don Q had managed to become an institution,
an underground icon, a symbol implanted in the subconscious
of the city. It stood unique in the heart of the streets, the windmill turning shadows through the sky by the spotlight cast
behind it, an image pasted in the memory of each patron who
had ever stumbled beneath its sails – every drinker in town had
a Don Q story to tell: the initiation of countless briefly legendary
bands into the music scene; the premiere of a play that went on
to become an independent film; the lovers who met there in pas-

sion and who no longer knew what had become of the other. Word of the Don Q's closing was an event to be both lamented and honored.

Romeo Díaz chose to focus on aspects of lamentation:

— You cannot do this to me, he moaned.

— Man, it's already done, claimed Beau.

— I will start drinking at home, threatened Romeo. I won't have any reason to leave the house.

— It's up to you.

— I'll be one of those people you get in the papers, nobody sees him except on runs to the liquor store, the kids are scared of him, and then one day he disappears. No one knows what happened to him until the police come to the house over neighbor complaints about stink, and they'll have to break in, and they'll find me decomposed after weeks, hidden under bottles and porn magazines. They'll identify me by dental records.

— You are your own man, counseled Beau.

Beau and Glenda took the route of honoring the memory of their great effort, and decided to celebrate the closing. They planned an all-day shindig, a hootenanny, an end-of-summer festival – with all relevant pagan connotations – to close down the show. There would be music from the local bands willing to say goodbye in forty-five-minute sets, short sketches by improv groups, an hour of poetry reading (*at most*, Glenda asserted, to placate Romeo). The newspaper covered what it called *this last bastion of sixties' values* and wished the Stileses well – though the editors were surely hoping, too, for more interesting drama: In his interview Beau let slip that officer Chesley Sutherland, one of those on paid leave while the city investigated the shooting death of Mather Williams, would play master of ceremonies overseeing the auction of mementos. The taps, the glasses, the ceramic-tiled bar with its mahogany frame, the antique light fixtures, even the bust of Cervantes and the framed photo of J. Edgar Hoover with meant everything to his future as a businessman and creative individual. An idea for a film. So Beau conceded feeling some concern about *that*. Otherwise his attitude was that the Don Q should go out with a bang.

— Let's have a night to remember, Beau said. We deserve it.

— I want good memories!

— You sound a lot like your mother right now.

A sore spot for Glenda, which Beau knew, and which ended the conversation right there.

§

The musicians arrived first, so the drinking began early. Unwashed longhairs in T-shirts and ripped jeans called for the kegs to be opened and the amps cranked up; soon the toasts were shouted rather than spoken, ranging from the traditional "may the road always rise to meet you" to "fucking Beau Stiles, man, fucking *Beau!*"; they plunged into the food. Chesley Sutherland arrived, sporting cool cop sunglasses and a rented tux, and immediately got down to sweating hard. His collar grew dark and his fingers fluttered in constant motion over some part of his body as he scratched against the starchy outfit, yet Beau was impressed with how quickly the musicians calmed down just from Sutherland's swollen presence. He did not appear in possession of a firearm, and this sight comforted Glenda. And he displayed a rare light side of his personality, throwing himself into the spirit of the day by introducing patrons as they passed beneath the swooping windmill. To unfamiliar faces Sutherland asked their names and how they liked to be addressed, then walked them from the foyer to the steps leading down to the parlor, announcing their enties to the gathering crowd as a royal servant announces his master's arrival at a grand ball. T' act encouraged the merriment and made Sutherland

— The Hoover picture and the fishnet mannequin legs, Beau. They are mine. Do not even take bids.

— You got it, answered Beau, happy to see the day starting so well.

Glenda glared at the bare backs of the two women swimming into the horde as she told Beau she had spotted Lambret straggling along the edges of the crowd gathered in the garden. Yes, she was certain it was him; she thought he was a girl at first, with that long black hair of his; but when she called out to him he did not appear to hear her, and she lost sight of the boy quickly.

— He wasn't huffing anything, was he? Beau asked.

— How would I know? Glenda said. I barely caught his face.

She thought he was maneuvering in his typicial indirect and noncommittal way, bothering no one, hardly even taking part. Was this a problem? Did Beau think the boy could be up to something? Should they worry?

— Glenda, the day is going well, everybody's having a good time, Beau cautioned, a touch of irritation in his voice. Why don't you have a good time too?

§

Everybody *did* appear to be enjoying themselves: Within two hours the Don Quixote was at capacity. The place grew hot and close, warmed by body heat and the sunlight weighing in through the glass atrium window-ceiling, the sun now at an angle that sent calm windmill shadow-lines over the interior below. Chesley Sutherland's deep baritone clamored from garbled PA speakers, taking bids and hammering a loud *sold!* before announcing the next band to play, though his words were largely unintelligible to anyone not in the Theatre Room. People were laughing, and a humid mist of smoke and vapor settled just below the ceilings, blanketing the crowds in soft light. The two police officers Sutherland had arranged for had little to pre-occupy them, keeping an eye on the small group of protesters against Sutherland's presence; this tattered group milled about the parking lot shouting slogans with half a heart, the chants dying as quickly as they began, as if they simply could not muster the righteousness. They contented themselves with holding placards that called for justice, and assured that the people were watching. They did not strive to block traffic or to keep anyone from entering the club. When asked, their leader explained that the police had made no announcements regarding their internal investigation of the shooting, nor of the FBI's investigation, so there was little else to do but wait and see. They were there to let the authorities know that they would not let the matter rest. *The people are watching,* he asserted again.

— As long as they just watch, said Beau, when he heard.

Anantha had been there for some time, arriving quietly, and too late to be announced by Sutherland. Contrary to Glenda's worries, she wore only jeans and a white blouse – nothing outrageous or suggestive – with her hair pulled back in an easy pony. Lambret recognized her first, cautiously curious about her companion, a large, burly figure of Sutherland proportions, but hard, with good skin and fine teeth and celebrity hair. He wore a black suit, black turtleneck, black shades, and none of this made him appear thinner or smaller. Lamb did not find the man even vaguely familiar. He did not smile; he implied easy violence; he turned out to be Anantha's escort/bodyguard/business manager, who went by the name of Jake. This, Anantha pointed out with weird glee, accenting a rhetorical "of course," was not his real name.

— Something Romeo never figured out is that no one in the industry he wants to make such an impact upon uses their real name, she said. Poor thing, he'll always be a gate-crasher.

She appraised Selena and Aria in their provocative outfits across the rooms with a bemused smile, the satisfied smile of one who has already made her mark and asserted her position in the world and now gazes upon the young upstarts straining to gain what she has already transcended. She told Beau she was there to say goodbye to the place and the people she would always love. She told them all how already she had ordered flowers renewed on Mather's grave, a garish look-at-me affair of lilies and carnations that adorned his plain footstone, the card signed by another hand *In fondest memory, your Miss Amanda*. She subscribed to a service that renewed the flowers once a month for the next year, and planned to visit his resting place the next day, Sunday, in full black mourning garb, veiled and everything, for Jake to film for a segment in a planned videography of her life: *The Love Inside Anantha Bliss.*

To Lambret she explained, now in the garden, that the movie would be an amalgam of fantasy and reality, with scenes of her at home going about the care of her plants, washing dishes and taking business calls, interspersed with brief interviews of her speaking directly to the camera, behind-the-scenes outtakes from her past videos, a kaleidoscope of money shots, et cetera; she wanted to present glimpses of her life before she became a star, too. The scene at Mather's grave would lend some emotional weight to the endeavor, to balance the sex scenes that were planned. Didn't Lamb think so?

Lambret smiled, softly, his smile betraying the first early lines to scrawl from his eyes.

— Mather will always have such a special place in my heart, Anantha continued. All my work, all of my accomplishments from today on, are in honor of his sweet soul. I will never forgive Romeo for allowing this to happen to him. Too busy looking for girls to work in this shoe-poor town, I guess.

The boy responded with a blank stare. She ruffled his hair with a playful swipe of one hand, telling him he looked fantastic, so much healthier. Had he quit huffing? (Yes, he had, at least for now.) Well, he was very fortunate for being so young still, he was able to bounce back so much faster than she would be able to, given the same predicament. Which brought up a subject she wanted to discuss with him. She was glad to see Lambret, of course, she was glad *on a personal level,* but this movie biography she was doing – how old was he now? Was he of legal age? Because she would like to show some footage from their "evening together" to give viewers a glimpse of where she had started, where she had struggled to come up from.

— Just a snip here and there, she explained. I'm actually not happy with how I look in that shoot, the lighting was too harsh and I wasn't working out like I am now; my body isn't very toned.

Lambret was seventeen and told her so.

— But would you be willing to sign something that says you're of age? Actually, that you were of age when we shot that night? Jake?

She called over her escort. He had papers at the ready, slipping them from out of his inside breast pocket.

— See, you sign this waiver then I'm clear, we can say you showed us proof of age or whatever, not that anyone's going to be inspecting too closely, but just in case. We can fake something.

— Do I get paid?

— My kind of man, Jake said, smiling for the first time, the smile flashing a diamond stud implanted in one front tooth.

— We can pay a fee if you like. Five hundred dollars, say. But you get that one fee, you can't have points on the movie or anything. Sorry hon, that stuff is out of my hands. But I would like to use you.

Five hundred dollars was more money than the boy had ever seen. Five hundred dollars was more than he had ever imagined holding in his hands at one time. Five hundred dollars – what could you do with that kind of money? He agreed to the amount quickly, and again Jake was called to, handing the money over to him in slick fifties pulled from a wallet in the same breast pocket as the legal papers. Five hundred dollars? Lambret asked. *Yes, I am of age.*

— I'm so glad how things work out! Anantha exclaimed. It's always so much more fun to deal with friends.

— Five hundred American dollars, Lambret repeated, quietly, almost to himself.

Romeo's voice came calling over the din of music, the other voices in the crowded garden, the short-lived chants of scattered protesters pacing outside the wooden fence. The three looked up to see him push his way through the people, sounding Amanda's name, smiling, waving. Selena followed with Aria on her lead, clasped at the neck, oblivious of stares.

He approached them with a mouth twitched by thin laughter, still waving as he closed in, saying *There's my old darling!* as he leaned in to kiss her cheek. Anantha's companion greeted him by pushing Romeo back to arm's length with an impressively gentle firmness.

— I'm just trying to say hello, Romeo said, We go back a long way, me and Anantha, I just wanted –

— I know who you are. You can speak with Anantha from right there.

Romeo stopped short. He took a second to consider the large man before him, situated between him and his old love. She waved to him from around Jake's shoulder, allowed herself a giggle. Selena and Aria stared at Anantha as though they had discovered treasure.

— Anantha I wanted to talk some business with you is all, I'm glad you got my invite, I was worried you'd changed your contact info. I haven't been able, I just wanted to say how proud I am at how well you're doing but see I have this idea, a great idea for a movie....

Again he tried to move around Jake, who again stretched out his impressive arm, planting it in Romeo's chest to keep him at the assigned distance. Romeo held up his hands to display his lack of threat and pushed forth in his effort to discuss this venture – one that would transform the course and stature of adult entertainment, he felt certain, he had an entire business plan and a new cinematic vision already prepared. Naturally with Anantha at its center.

— And your two pets here, I imagine? Anantha asked.

— Bitch, Aria muttered in a heavy Eastern European accent, to the skies.

— *Mister* Bitch to you, honey, answered Anantha.

If you would just listen, Romeo urged on, moving toward Anantha, only to be pushed away again by big Jake in sunglasses. He flashed the diamond star of his teeth again.

Lambret was too preoccupied to pay any of them much attention. He turned his back and fingered the new bills, marveling at the weight of them in his hand, surprised at the heft of such few slips of paper. He returned and patted Anantha's arm as thanks, to which she merely nodded, too engrossed in enjoying the sight of Romeo's struggles and the self-consciousness of the two women to bother with the boy anymore – and Lambret understood. With Romeo there he knew the scene had changed to a story that did not include him. Even at his young age he understood that to Anantha he was nothing more than a business transaction. And that was how the world *worked*; Anantha did not owe him anything. Lambret moved off into the throng as though he had briefly slipped through a thin portal to glimpse himself in the culture of adults. He heard Romeo's voice rise high in outrage, the voice quickly fading behind him: *She loved me once, man,* Romeo cried, *Is this necessary?*

§

By dusk the crowd spilled into the avenue out front, to the gravel parking lot peppered by tiring protesters, to the back alley where Haycraft's living room had once stretched out its welcoming old sofas. No one seemed to be tiring; the day was gaining momentum. A hot August night punctuated by brief buffeting breezes – enough to animate the windmill, its sails groaning with each turn, exposing an abandoned bird's nest that rested over the center axle. Titmice and pigeons circled and returned, circled and returned, skittering sentinels squatting on the roof-top gutters.

Haycraft Keebler secreted himself into the crowd through the garden gate. He had lost a good deal of weight on the success of the all-potato diet, and had disguised himself this night with a coquette bob wig, full mascara, and lipstick smeared across his mouth and stubbled chin, his body draped in a dress poorly sewn from what appeared to be two dresses of contrasting prints. Only the indispensable sandals and familiar oilcloth satchel betrayed him. Stray papers spilled behind as he steered sharply through the people, thrusting about the new edition of his *Fair Dealer* into the hands of anybody willing to accept one. After which each face inspecting the page would crimp into bewilderment or indifferent laughter. In minutes the papers found their way to the floor, carpeting a path in Haycraft's wake before he had even made it to the bar, one of Sutherland's officers trailing not far behind.

— On the grave of your father, Glenda sighed.

— Holy damn, Beau let slip at the sight, recognizing the churlish face demanding an ale.

Glenda's hand shot to her forehead as if to cross herself, then hesitated as she thought better of it, her face transforming from a kind of frightful shock to a twisted neighbor of relief, then abbreviated laughter; the hand, a nervous sparrow, smoothed back her hair.

But Haycraft was not interested in comedy. He slapped his hand on the bar and declared:

— Betrayers! Deceivers! The last I expected to remove their shoulders from the wheel! You have humiliated us all. A pint, please.

— It's okay, Beau told the officer glowering behind Hay,

reaching from between two patrons to yank him from the floor. He's one of ours.

— I have much more to say, Haycraft continued, then didn't.

He had thinned dramatically. Beau handed him a glass with eyes inviting explanations. Glenda seemed able only to stare. Soon she recovered by expressing "everyone's" worry over his whereabouts, his health, his happiness or not – she pinched the shoulder of his dress and shook her head: How much weight had he lost? *You look so pale,* she cried.

Haycraft did not respond, too busy shoveling out newsletters to the bevy of onlookers who groused nearby, snickering at him. He smiled in return, a smile revealing a mouth shorn of three teeth, and danced his head. Only when his hand had emptied did he turn back to her:

— A complication directly related to my diet, he explained. Apparently no matter how many different ways one can prepare a potato, it seems to still lack certain necessary nutritional values. I've been forced to allow myself certain amenities in preparation of this spectacular night but the effects have yet to show.

He sucked down his ale in three long gulps, the loose, shave-reddened turkey-waddle of skin at his throat jerking with each swallow. Finished, he cracked the empty glass hard on the bar tiles and motioned for another.

— Mather is dead, you know. But of course you know, we can see you've hired one of his assassins to anchor your celebration.

— Oh, Haycraft, Glenda began; she was unable to come up with any further response and then sought help from her husband. Beau?

— I have spent my forty days in the wilderness, Beau! I have seen the tiger's smile, I have wrestled with the devil!

— And lost, Romeo interrupted, clapping a hand on Haycraft's back. His jejune leer was perhaps an honest attempt at camaraderie and warmth, his best effort possible with heart and pride smarting after more failures with his Amanda. She had allowed him to grovel for some time before informing Jake that enough was enough; she had given Romeo nothing. With a sniff Selena drew Aria away and out of the garden on her chain, and for some long moments Romeo stood there alone, abandoned by everyone.

— It's good to have you back, Hay. Even, even looking like this. We have all really missed you.

— I appreciate your candor, Romeo. You have never been far from my thoughts. Enlightenment values, progressive thinkers, we share a common humanity that all have lost sight of, individuals struggling through the herd. We are linked, you and I, we are different but *linked* (yes, I have thought, critiqued, analyzed this from every perceivable angle!), whereas you pull inward I reach outward, we still both wish for the world to be a place different from what it is.

He handed Romeo a copy of the *Fair Dealer*'s latest edition. The entire paper was composed of a single article in four pages of eight-point, three-column print, entitled "Janus: The State and Society as Androgynous Entities." *Good people of our fair district,* the essay began:

> now is the time for our wildest imaginings and most fervent commitment. The time has come to stave the masculine ego of our society, the progressive striving to differentiate ourselves from – and yet also control – this edifice-like matrix from which we have emerged. So much of it is all just violence and battle. The time has come to embrace the feminine principles, to reunite with the mystery of life, of nature, of soul and community. I, Haycraft Keebler, humble servant of our sacred yet oppressed Old Towne, wish to express to you the revelations that have been rained down

upon me as the representative of our community to
the mystical powers of our presumably indifferent
universe that wish to guide the affairs of all
humankind by mere example....

Romeo set down the paper on the tiles of the bar. Haycraft was
humming already, clenching and unclenching his fists as his
head wheeled over the thinned neck, somehow spying the entire
room, somehow winking at everyone there as if they were all in
on his own private joke.

Romeo told Haycraft to drink up, to have another on him: *Yes,
I'm buying the drinks again, Hay!*

— Hey, you know what? I want to apologize; yeah, *listen* I
want to make up for all the ways I've hurt you, he added, almost
modestly.

— Hurt? Why no, Romeo, what you did was show me in
explicit light the desultory apathy I'd allowed myself, foolishly, to
be captivated by, focusing my energies on a single boy when it's
the entire community that requires my attentions. It is Sutherland
who has hurt me most, the Chesley Sutherlands of the world
who have hurt us all. And there is no more time to talk, do not
stress yourself, it is time to allow deeds to speak for words.

— Do you know you aren't talking sense, man? Do you know
you don't talk sense at all?

— Ha! Ha ha ha ha! Sense! But I am so *sensitive!*

Hay's laughter had nothing merry in it; each laugh came as
insult, hurtful to the ears. He was sweating mascara.

— For all my talk of developing lunar and Dionysian consciousness as a worldview for the people, I'd allowed myself to be
coaxed into a personal relationship that relied exclusively on the,
hmmmmm, Apollonian principle....

— Lambret? asked Glenda. Hay, are you speaking of Lambret?
He's here, honey. I saw him.

— He's not!

But Beau and Romeo concurred. Yes, they had all seen him, skirting the verge of the crowd, talking with Anantha and her guard. At this news, Haycraft sank to silence. He adjusted his wig, wiped at a run of mascara that traced a forking path down one cheek. He aired his dress from beneath the armpits, pulling it away from his chest, and Romeo stepped back.

— For the best, for the best of everyone, Haycraft continued, suddenly. I have a few of his friends hidden about the grounds, I should warn you. Tonight shall be our great unveiling, hmmm? Our reckoning, as it were. And the boy; as I have planned it all for him – in a sense, yes *sense*, Romeo! There is your word again! – he *should* be here rather than learning of it all secondhand. He should be here, bearing witness to this moral crime – you still have Mather's paintings arranged over your walls, I see. Tell me, are they for sale, too? Are you having Sutherland take bids for Mather's work?

Beau had no time to answer before Haycraft swept his girth from the stool, beer glass aslosh in hand, and pushed against the wall of bodies forming the edge of the crowd.

— The microphone! Please allow me the floor, Beau, for a few moments only –

At first the people resisted him, but against Hay's persistence soon parted willingly enough. Beau ordered Romeo to keep an eye on the man and Romeo hurried after, intense in the wash that widened behind.

They headed up the brief tiled stairs and launched themselves into the confusion of the Theatre Room, where the so-called assassin Chesley Sutherland held sway. On the rear of the stage a band was at work connecting their guitars to the back line, testing volume, and taking their positions as Sutherland paced the foreground reciting bad jokes about protesters that few could hear; he tried to tell quick stories in the familiar bar-room style, in the staccato cadences of the present tense – but all the crowd wanted from him was to run the auction. He banged a mallet hammer on the wood of the stage floor to close the bidding on a potted fern. *Sold!* he shouted, and mimed applause. Then he set about inspecting the stacks of things for sale, rummaging through appliances and picture frames, settling on one and returning to the front of the stage.

Haycraft watched, open-mouthed in awesome disbelief. His hand found Romeo's shoulder and slowly increased into a tight grip; the noise of talk and laughter and skidding chairs faded as Sutherland opened bidding on a Mather Williams canvas.

— Impossible, Haycraft whispered.

He knew the picture – it was called "The Heart of the City," a title bestowed by Glenda, because the pastel and ink rendition of urban architecture was arranged in a way that reminded her of a rib cage; the street down its center pulsed with cardiac red.

Haycraft left Romeo and muscled his bulk to the stage, his glass held before him as a priest with chalice approaches the altar. Foamy beer sloshed over his hands and braided down his forearms.

— Outrage, I beg you to stop! he pleaded, gesturing at the microphone.

Sutherland reacted with a face of polite inquiry, an ingrained good-boy solicitousness to any entreating old heavy woman. Then he recognized the man in wig and split-print dress. He turned away and displayed, suddenly, an acute interest in the band waiting patiently behind him. Auction abandoned. Haycraft repeated his call, and was this time completely ignored. Repeated it again. As he started into yet another appeal Sutherland responded, this time with more mild finesse; a lifting of eyebrows and screwed shoulders indicating he could not hear the man for the noisy crowd, the drummer testing his snare. Acting as though he had only realized Haycraft's presence just now.

Invoking the spirit of town-hall civic meetings and timeless common fellowship, Haycraft broached the stage with a shout.

Chesley's eyes widened; he backpedaled into a heavy stack of amplifiers and pressed the microphone against his chest. *No,* he barked once, biting off the word as in disciplining a small child. *Not now, later!*

But Haycraft was on a mission.

Chesley shouted, *The band is about to start!*

— Well yes but I have something to say, Haycraft stated. You can't deny me the right, I have the tide of the horde at my back. Artful terrorists surround you! They only await my command.

Chesley scanned the crowd in the Theatre Room, eyes tight and crimped. His two policemen were nowhere to be found.

— The protesters are all outside, he reasoned.

— Never underestimate the powers of disguise, as you must now know having seen through my little masquerade. The time has come for the people's voice to be heard!

Romeo joined them on the stage. He gripped the hem of Hay's dress to restrain the man, whispering to him the mantra of *later, later Haycraft, it's a long night and we have plenty of time, you must be patient,* Romeo grasping Haycraft gently across the shoulder to guide him away. *Let me buy you another beer, you've spilled that one.* Then he added: *You don't want to ruin the night for Beau and Glenda, do you.*

The words were enough to convince Hay to come away. For the moment.

The band launched into a set that recast the crowd into a thriving body: Around Haycraft the stomping turned wild and the bodies and heads bobbed furiously, as if lashed by invisible yet squalling waves. Haycraft glared at the twisting, sweaty forms, the flying hair; he licked froth from his mustache with indignant revulsion. He railed against the madness of selling Mather's memory, yet just as soon he seemed to let the matter drop, and fell silent, exuding impatience. In a continual cycle of motion he checked a watch on his hip that was not there; he had no belt loop to string a watchband through. Shuffling in the foyer, he urged Romeo to help him spot the provocateurs. *But I don't know what you're talking about,* Romeo said.

—Now is our *time*, we can make a *statement* that the city will hear. Tonight we have an audience, Mather cannot be swept under, he was real and he had love and someone must make example of the Chesley Sutherlands –

— What have you got planned, Hay? What are you up to?

— I don't quite know ... but I do! I do know all right, Haycraft said, then burst into wild laughter until he could control himself enough to blurt: You see that it all makes such *perfect sense!*

Romeo gripped both of Haycraft's arms square before him, staring up into the eyes huge behind thick lenses, as if there he could discern what was coming. He may as well have consulted a blank screen for news of the world; the eyes gave nothing. He heard Haycraft's feckless laugh and wondered humming; saw Hay's fingers flutter against one another with palms pressed together before him. Romeo did not press further; soon the band ended their set and the crowd surged high in applause.

It was the instant Haycraft had been waiting for.

He bolted into the Theatre Room and for the microphone. Chesley made it there before him, and the harangue began again: *Good Chesley! A moment with the microphone, please!* and *No!* and *Please, a moment only,* and *Go away!*

Titters of laughter tweaked the crowd as the battle intensified. Voices chimed in: *Let him talk!* and others: *Sit down, you freak!* The heat in the room rose, pushed forward on waves of sweat and cigarette smoke; Haycraft pulled at the front of his dress to allow his torso some air. Yet he remained focused on his goal. As Sutherland tried to pitch a lame joke, Hay again broached the stage, one hand held out imploringly. Again laughter swept from the crowd, and now the overhead fan-lights twittered on loose connections as people stomped their feet. Chesley tried to move away, Haycraft chasing, his whirling satchel knocking a cymbal stand. Chesley darted behind the drum kit; he feinted one way then the other, daring Haycraft to commit himself, so that they were soon chasing one another in a circle around a bewildered drummer who had sat down to begin his set. The crowd was roaring by the time Romeo stepped in, hugging Haycraft at the belly despite the powerful odor emanating from him – a mix of asparagus and old cooking oil.

Chesley saw the chance to end the comedy. The next band stood ready and waiting, checking sound levels as though nothing else were going on around them. Wiping his wet brow with the sleeve of his tux, Chesley pantomimed a called truce. He raised the microphone gently to his lips.

— Ladies and gentlemen, I ask here for a moment of audience participation, he announced, flourishing his left hand in a theatrical gesture at invitation. Okay folks, what we got is a man many of you know but probably more of you don't, for which you ought to be thankful. I say he's the one responsible for the gold junk we got all around town. He wants to speak to you about something, I don't know, the social problems of Old Towne or whatever. Me, I want to party in Beau and Glenda's honor ... but I am a fair man, and he's pretty pumped up and I figure you all can either let him speak or else allow your next band here – (His eyes dropped to a scrap of paper scrawled with handwriting) – *The Horizontal Pipelayers*. Let's hear what everyone thinks. All in favor of our speaker say Aye.

A smattering of voices rose in unison, along with clapping hands. Haycraft surveyed the crowd with pride. He beamed with hard-won triumph. His heavy foot again thudded on the stage, mushrooming plumes of dust about his ankle.

— All in favor of this wondrous band whose legendary sound has returned from the past for our simple enjoyment?

The crowd howled with excitement. Empty beer cups rained

onto both Chesley and Haycraft, who did nothing to protect himself from them. Chesley leaned in, smiling. He spoke again, within hearing of the microphone:

— Sorry buddy. The people have spoken.

The crowd bayed and wailed again as the drummer marched into a boom-chicka rhythm. Chesley Sutherland moved to one side, not yet off the stage, clapping his hands in time, still in the lights ...

... and Haycraft was not finished. Almost thoughtfully, he raised one hand above his head and snapped his fingers in a strange, flamenco-like gesture, oddly graceful in such a large, awkward man. At that instant two boys bolted from the back of the room to the stage. Romeo Díaz would say he heard Haycraft shout *Justice!*, and it is true that Hay was pointing in the direction of Sutherland at the time. But the band was in full throttle now, and the action happened quickly enough that no one had the opportunity to stop the boys from closing in on Sutherland; Chesley himself only registered the attack as the two set upon him, arms raised.

They made quick, efficient work of it. Sutherland dropped to one knee, shielding himself too late from the offensive against him. He cried out as the blows took him in the face and head, splashing over the tuxedo and floor, Sutherland falling quickly – crumpling, really – onto the stage, his body shellacked by hurled pies.

The boys kept running past their victim and into the night out the open windows, a loud bang of a heel against the pine windowsill and an echoing epithet, a holler trailed by room-wide laughter. The band played on, the drummer adding a Vegas roll-and-snap to his beat.

Yet the moment was not over. Haycraft approached Sutherland as if to help him; but as he neared the fallen man, his hand – rather than reaching forward in aid – reached behind, disappearing into the satchel at his hip. As Sutherland raised to his hands and knees, Haycraft raised one leg and pressed his sandaled foot down into Chesley's shoulder, forcing him down again, grinding his cheek into the dusty slats of the makeshift stage.

— For Mather, for Old Towne, but most of all, for me, Haycraft sneered into the meringue of Sutherland's exposed ear, pinned beneath his foot.

He slung his hand from the satchel gripping a weapon of some kind, already shooting before anyone could react. His arm shook with the force of the discharge, or with rage.

Romeo responded quickly, tackling Haycraft from behind, sending both men into the kick drum. The band screeched to a halt among the clatter of fallen cymbals and brief shear of feedback as the guitarist backed into his amp. Everyone else stood still in shock. And there, in that short pocket of time before the shouting started, only a single sound rang clear: the bell-ring wobble of a spray can settling onto the stage.

Everyone looked; they peered over the shoulders of others to survey the outcome. Chesley Sutherland's sweating head shone distinct beneath the smoky stage lights, encased in gold.

§

Romeo got Haycraft to his feet and hustled him to the nearest door as the crowd rushed the stage. The closest one he found left them in the dark of one of the building's back rooms.

— Now that was a rather bold move, Romeo said. I wouldn't have guessed you had it in you.

There was almost respect in Romeo's voice; a warmth at the bottom of it. Haycraft detected the change though he felt dazed, disoriented; he tottered uncertainly from one foot to the other as his sight made its way through the shadows. His humming silenced itself and he swallowed, loudly. He listened for a moment to the sounds that he had left behind: scraping chairs, a shout, the gabber and holler of drunks. The mob he had so much to say to, and who did not want to hear him. There they were, on the other side of that door: the people on one side, him on the other. Haycraft Keebler, Lord of Old Towne alleyways, their Napoleon in Rags, walled off from his own efforts.

— Do you know what they are doing in there right now, just beyond that door? Haycraft asked, his cheek near the lime, sunken paneling, hand on brass knob. Helping Sutherland to his feet. They are helping him *recover from his attack*. People, they see a man go down, see him *attacked*, and what do they do, they try to help. Even if this is the same man who, if they thought about it, brought so much sorrow to their own lives. Why do they help *him* now? That's what I've never understood, Romeo; people *want* to help one another. After a fashion. But where were they when Mather needed someone? When Lamb and his friends are on the street? It's the strangest thing, you can show a man how to change his world, and he'll end up feeding a wild dog simply because it's a stray.

To this, Romeo had nothing to add. He tried to set his face in a mode of compassion – a difficult and alien settling of his features, one that he was not accustomed to making and that he was not certain he knew *how* to make. But it did not really matter; Haycraft was not looking at him, and it was too dark to see one another's faces distinctly.

The outrage, the disrespect, Haycraft stammered as he stumbled in the darkness. Startled by the grunt of a skidding stool, the hollow *dong* of empty plastic jars tumbling to the floor, he cried out. Again Romeo settled him; in the dim light crossing a fogged window, the teeth of his smile shone blue. He said to Haycraft:

— Slow down, take it easy, we don't want to break any of Beau's stuff.

The statement gave Haycraft pause; abruptly he fell into thought. But only for a brief instant.

— *Beau's stuff....* Another outrage, that. An outrage to my father's memory, I tell you. Do you know where we are, Romeo?

Romeo took in the darkness and considered.

— The storage room?

— No. The *card* room. This was the parlor, you see. Here the men played poker while I pushed my toy trucks under their table, over their feet. This room smelled of cigars and leather and dust in the rug. Now (here he raised his face and sniffed noisily in the air), there's nothing. Old brick, crumbled mortar.

Haycraft pulled off his wig, spat into his hand. He began to rub at his face vigorously. He slumped his hips onto a long steel-topped table, and sighed a loud, gushing mass of air, almost a moan.

— I don't understand. How does one make a difference? How do you make a public statement, effect change, without it all turning to farce? I have made a farce of everything, Romeo.

— Hay, I *live* a farce, and let me tell you it has its own satisfactions. You think Sutherland saw us come in here?

Haycraft shrugged him away with a motion of his hand, the hand holding the wig.

— I'm not going anywhere. There is still more for me to do.

He stood up again from the table, pushing off with his hips.

— It's a difficult task, you know. Very difficult to incite the people; to lead them where they don't want to be led. And yet they are so quick to tell you how dissatisfied they find their lives. *Save me*, I hear them saying. But they don't want to be saved, Romeo.

— That's the sanest thing I've heard from your mouth in a long time, Hay.

Immediately Haycraft retreated from the sane thing. His next statement made no sense to Romeo, who watched the door to the Theatre Room, waiting for Sutherland to burst through with his pair of quislings sporting handcuffs. Haycraft spoke low:

— It's just part of the story, isn't it? You are all simply characters in my story, and I have to realize I have no control of that.

His voice had an edgy, unsettling calm.

— What do you mean? Romeo asked.

— You. Beau. Glenda, Lambret, Mather. Even Chesley Sutherland, who just confirmed himself as my Pilate.

Romeo looked down at his feet in the darkness.

— I see how my story will be written. The form it will take in the imagination of others.

Now Romeo, never a patient man, frowned. He had no idea what Haycraft was going on about and he felt a great need to hurry the man away, if he could find a way out. He did not understand what Haycraft was after; only that he seemed misguided, a bit *off*, in danger of pulling himself out of reality – out of Romeo's reality, at least. Which was the same as it ever was and therefore unsurprising.

— Haycraft, do you know how to get out of here?

— The only way out is up. Which suits our needs perfectly, I would say. I do appreciate your help in giving me this respite, Romeo. Now come along, I want to show you something that just happens to be on the way.

Romeo followed as Haycraft groped his way past the edges of tables and shelves to a stairwell at the far side of the room, where the shadows of a half-dozen steps disappeared into total darkness.

— Be careful, Romeo cautioned. I can't see a damn thing.

— I can stroll up these steps in my sleep. In fact I often do, walking this house in my dreams, Haycraft muttered, then promptly tripped and spilled himself over the stairs, filling his nose with dust. He sneezed once, twice; he pulled a handkerchief from somewhere deep under his dress.

— Well, Haycraft said. They seem to have narrowed.

— Put your hands against the walls, they'll guide you.

Haycraft did, and the two men together moved up the rickety stairwell, curious children exploring a vacant, abandoned building, hearts and adrenaline pumping with the expectation of possible discoveries – coupled with the vague fear of being caught.

— Hay, where are you taking me? Romeo asked, his voice hushed.

— We're here, Haycraft answered. We are home.

At the top of the stairs Haycraft rested, catching his breath. His eyes – those weak muscles of perception – required long moments to adjust to changes in light, and the only faint light in these rooms flattened against the long double-hung windows at the farthest side from the stairwell, across the wretched and worn room, facing the nighttime street. Haycraft sneezed again. Below, the noise of the crowd in the Theatre Room seemed to sweep up behind them on the stairwell, only to be shushed again by the slamming of the door. A voice bellowed Keebler's name.

— Sutherland's here, Romeo whispered.

Haycraft nodded. He seemed hardly aware of anyone now. Fallen into a kind of nostalgic wonder, he brushed past Romeo and toward the windows, his feet scattering a sharp rattling pile of empty beer bottles. The two men stilled until the bottles ran to a stop. Then Hay lay one hand briefly over a mishmash stack of cardboard boxes, dragging his finger through the film of dust clinging to the topmost. Below him the floorboards vibrated with the hard beat of the drums starting in again downstairs; a howl of feedback clawed the air and then abruptly stopped. But in these rooms it all seemed very far away, lost beneath the tingling, acrid bite of settled ash, the sodden rotting wood and mortar, cobwebs, Haycraft's sweating body. He pressed his nose against the leaded glass of the far window; he placed his palms against the coolness of it, a child gazing into a store full of favorite toys.

— Do you know what I'm going to tell you, he began.

— Keebler, you up there? I am here for you, Sutherland announced from the bottom of the stairwell, through the damp and dark.

Haycraft tilted his head, but otherwise did not respond. His breath fogged the window before him, and he wiped the mist away with the hem of his dress. Speaking low again to Romeo, he began to murmur a story: of how this floor had once been three rooms – here he moved to indicate the remains of wall frames, bashed through some time ago by vandals, exposing the lathes and the clotted guts of gypsum board and plaster. As the sound of Sutherland's hesitant bootfalls made its way up the stairwell, Romeo backed from the opening and into the deeper darkness. But Hay stood in one naked doorframe.

— This one, here, was my bedroom. I grew up in this very spot, you see, he said. It was very safe, my childhood.

It had been a childhood rife with ambition and ideals (*our very walls hummed with the two; this was a place for hopeful dreaming*) Haycraft told Romeo, who tried to pay attention but could not avoid the cry of a thousand seagulls in Chesley's breath as he neared. It was a very happy period for him, Haycraft continued. For a time. Until it went away, he said. *Until it was taken away.* And now the closing of the Don Q was like losing his home once again.

— Even if it appears that, for a brief period at least, I'd become again a new, *transformed* prodigal son. I needed time to go away and think, do you understand, Romeo? To speak to my own devils. And now twice I have lost my place for dreaming.

Sutherland now stood in the dark at the top of the stairs, bent slightly, his hands clenched on his thighs. He coughed a shallow cough, a retching from the throat as though his chest could not be opened. He hawked and spat on the floor.

— Ah you can dream all you want where I'm taking you, he croaked. You'll have nothing to do but sit and dream.

— Chesley, you are not welcome here, Romeo warned.

— I'm never welcome anywhere unless I'm needed, Díaz. Come on, Hay, we want you downstairs.

Haycraft did not move. He stood in the doorframe to his old bedroom, staring, his back to both men. Sutherland stepped closer, until Romeo stopped him with his shoulder – a light obstruction, two men bumping one another on a sidewalk, nothing more. Romeo could hear the whistling in the big man's lungs.

— Your head is glowing, Chesley. Nice touch, now that I think about it, how it catches the glow off the streetlights.

Sutherland's response was composed of a single thrust of his arm into Romeo's chest, briefly pinning him against the wall. Curling waves of dust broke out around his body and covered both men, forcing Sutherland to back off a step and wipe his eyes, set him to coughing hard again. Haycraft approached them before anything more could happen between the two.

— This fucking paint, I think I'm allergic to it, Sutherland panted.

— I'm ready to go, Haycraft announced over the snuffling. Through here, follow me, I'll show you the easiest way down. You need clean, open air, Chesley.

— Just come on, Hay, let's go back the way I came, listen, I'm not as angry like you think I am. I'm going to get you some help, Chesley said, his voice dried to a thin cheeping, clearing his throat and spitting again.

— I appreciate that, Chesley. I do. But let's go through this way. In reality it is I who am trying to help you.

— Help me?

— Indeed, help *you*, he repeated.

Suddenly Haycraft seemed so confident, beneficent, nearly papal; he was not so close as to be within Sutherland's reach, but still was welcoming to both men, acting with the airs of a comforted and comforting host. Now Haycraft was leading them – and Romeo was shocked to see Chesley Sutherland, sucking hard on his asthma inhaler, numbly following. They broached another broken staircase, a path lit by the ghostly hues of a hard moon breaking through slats in the ceiling, the walls. They cleared their way through repeated veils of spiderwebs. And Haycraft was speaking again, launching into another of his winding lectures, this one woven from unlikely references to the fates of Socrates, Jesus, Kepler and Copernicus and Galileo. The point gradually becoming clear that their unwanted trials and martyrdoms had led to epochal transformation.

— Even Nietzsche! he blurted out as they reached the tar-paper eaves of the roof, where the district of Old Towne stretched to downtown Montreux, and to the unseen river behind, blocked by the canyon walls of office buildings.

— Perhaps now, in my own small, humble way, the turn is mine, he added.

Wielding an unworldly air, he raised his right hand in a gesture that simultaneously indicated their modest Canaan and blessed it.

— *Breathe*, Chesley, breathe deeply! He prompted, leering a comic smile, miming with his own body deep intakes of breath, filling his lungs and exhaling loudly. Then he waved his hand over the city again.

— All this I prepare for you, Haycraft announced. All this I give to you. Take it, keep it, and remember me.

With these words he wavered somewhat in the light breeze that felt cool over each of them after the humidity of the bar. Romeo and Sutherland stood beside one another, remaining at the mouth of the skewed stairwell for fear of falling over the broken planes of cinder and tar. They watched and did not move as Haycraft braved his way to the far edge of the roof toward the garden side of the building, upsetting a roost of fat pigeons that took to the sky on a loud whoosh of wings and vocal complaints, wheeling viciously into the sky in a widening, nervous spiral, refusing to return while Haycraft remained.

Haycraft ignored them; he stopped behind the creaking wind-mill, steadying one hand against the old iron hub. He looked down, over the edge.

— What are you up to, Hay? Sutherland asked.

Romeo tried to go to him, but with his first step Sutherland had him by the shoulder, keeping him from moving further.

— Romeo? asked Hay. I would ask a favor of you. Please keep an eye out for the welfare of Lambret. Explain to him what I have done. He is a delicate boy.

He raised his arms and started to sway, moving as a member in a Baptist congregation, lost in his faith, waving. Before him, the decrepit windmill began to turn with its sharp, cracking aches; the pigeons returned, bobbling nearby, fluttering atop one of the three chimneys. A crowd of murmuring voices, ignorant of the drama above, laughing, rose from the garden. Romeo told Sutherland they needed to do something. Again Romeo started toward the edge but Sutherland held him back.

— Hell, Hay, what are you up to? Sutherland shouted.

— Haycraft, come off the ledge, Romeo said.

— Fear not! Haycraft boomed back. Good friends, every new age needs its martyr! I have tried, I have searched, and it is apparent that this soul is to be my own. Be silent, please, and appreciate the gravity of this moment.

Romeo would later say that he did not understand a word Haycraft spoke this night; that, although in retrospect it seemed the three of them stood there on the roof among the nests and stars for a very long time, at the moment it seemed to be happening very fast. Sutherland would state that he was dazed from lack of oxygen due to his asthma attack and all the stairs, and his eyes still burned from where the gold paint had hit them; that when he realized Haycraft's determination, it was already too late. No one but these three knew exactly what happened on that rooftop, or how it happened, but what is certain is that Haycraft shouted *Redeem yourselves, O lost!* as he stepped up onto the hub of the windmill and over the edge, into the air.

NOTES
TOWARD
AN
ENDING

THE DON QUIXOTE IS JUST ANOTHER piece of city history now. An empty husk and occasion of lore, rarely bandied about by the voices in the smaller, smokier, less ambitious taverns around town. There are still working music groups who got their start there, who dutifully mention the place on their media kits or on-air interviews. Now they reference Beau and Glenda's place as *The Legendary Don Quixote*. Local drama troupes lament its demise as they search doggedly for performance spaces; the alcoholics have all found their own new favorite watering holes, as they are required to do. But for those who met there regularly, who ate, drank, teased and shouted, sang with the jukebox or else stared dumbly at the silent TV, the Don Q is gone and there is no reason to be together anymore. Without that central web, its sticky strands pulling them in day after day onto the tired stools at the bar, they no longer held anything in common; they were released upon their own paths.

Beau and Glenda are now fairly old. Their son Damon does

the legwork for the remains of their catering business. They continue to make their house payments by renting out the attic as an apartment. Damon is a common player in the variety of community theaters around the city, acting in basements and old storefronts. None of the regulars have ever ventured to any of his performances.

Romeo Díaz perseveres in his battle with the Ruin, and the neighborhood. He wanders draped in a long macintosh worn even in summer, topped by a fedora hat, the edge tipped downward at a rakish angle. He insists men's fashion ended after the 1940s. He is officially on hiatus from all fiascoes, but has opened his own adult bookstore/anarchist literature distribution center (cinematic booths in the back operated by fifty-cent tokens). He moonlights as estate-curator of Mather Williams' works, which have received a good deal of interest from regional collectors. Mather's illustrations grace the covers of CDs by local bands, and hang in the scattering of coffeehouses, the occasional gallery. Romeo hopes to publish a monograph retrospective one day, funded in part by the movie he still hopes to make starring Anantha Bliss. A *real* movie, he says, with feature-film quality – none of this video stuff – and with a *real* story and acting, along with full XXX action. He claims Anantha has expressed interest, and that he no longer has to speak to her through the intermediary of a larger man's fist staved against his chest. Romeo looks upon this development as progress. Still, nearly twelve years since the closing of the Don Quixote, we have yet to hear of an actual shooting date. They have yet to find the right script, according to Romeo. He worries that Anantha, aging well but still aging, is no longer the bright star of the industry she once was.

He never asks about Haycraft, not on the off-times we run into one another downtown. Nor does he inquire of me.

§

Haycraft Keebler, our supposed savior, our self-proclaimed community martyr, did not die from his rooftop leap that cool summer night. No doubt he intended to, but often Hay became rapt by the symbolic nature of a gesture and did not consider the objective ramifications. The Don Quixote was only an old farm-house after all, not quite three true stories high. Perhaps in Haycraft's mind the monumental significance he projected onto the place made it seem a mighty height. But his attempt at cruel martyrdom succeeded only in covering his body with cuts and bruises, cracked ribs, more lost teeth, and a shattered hip. And the act – maybe this goes without saying – did not inspire the masses to revolt and secede, or even to recognize their implicit freedom to ruin their own lives. It did not usher in the new age where the masculine and feminine principles have married and balanced in the State, producing a whole-some independence in the people. In fact his action changed nothing at all.

Except me. I cared for him through his last years, along with my wife. Haycraft led a much quieter life after that day, and, weeks later, his subsequent return home from the city hospital – although his mouth did always retain that peculiar shape of a life-affirming *yes* about to be spoken. He became more diligent (through our influence) in keeping to his helpful medications; he turned less prone to the grandiloquent orations, and was more likely to confess only a mordant confusion at other people's behavior – most of which he encountered through the television set. He watched the news channels in twelve-hour intervals, no longer consulting the moon nor its phases nor its supposed codes. After his fall he required a cane to move around, a necessity he did not like (Haycraft was still a proud man). He preferred to have me run the daily errands required by every household, no matter how small. His political activism dwindled to attaching his name to ballots for local elections, but he cut back his campaigning to the placement of classified ads, which stated he would hold weekly civic meetings open to the public, if elected. There was no more talk of secession; there was very little talk at all. He did not write anymore, not even the most meager letter to the editor. Even when the pneumonia was ready to take him two years ago, when he asked for a notebook and pen so that he could write down some kind of final thoughts, he ended up leaving only blank pages behind.

And me? I am no longer the boy Lambret Dellinger. I have changed my name and my life. No longer do I frequent the park at night, sidling by the graffitied statue of Haycraft's forgotten father in search of an easy trick; I am no longer a hazy teenager scared to make his presence known among adults. I would have difficulty explaining the boy I was then. Certainly there is some psychologist who could gladly theorize a number of informed reasons as to why that is, but I don't need any answers. It is enough to have realized, in setting down this story, that transformations are possible – if only on the small scale of one simple and obscure life. As Haycraft always said – and Glenda, too – we suffer from a lack of willingness to imagine the experience of others. It is in their honor that I have reimagined this story and written down all of what I could access.

I find myself visiting the building often, the place abandoned now, owned by a city that never could find a use for it. I walk the grounds and try a variety of angles from which to gaze at the old farmhouse that made me, where the windmill still runs its haphazard compass; it creaks weakly in the sporadic breeze, then shocks with an abrupt, cracking shot. The battered sails are hollowed by squirrels and inhabited by birds that paint the boards with streaks of white and slops of green. I think it should be recognized; it should be renovated. We should have it refinished in a patina of gold.

I consider the site and ignore the calls for money from the men with their hands out, the babbling conversation of old women pushing grocery carts, the halfhearted come-ons from the neighborhood girls getting an early start to their workday. It is easy to ignore the plunging cries of sirens and those omnipresent vascular lights, to overlook the flashing red and doppler blue. Yes, a broken windmill preserved in gold – gold paint to transform the splintering, decayed wood into art, into a monument. A monument, perhaps, for myself only; as a way to remember how really very little a man can do to change the world.

ACKNOWLEDGMENTS

The author would like to thank the editors at *The Southeast Review*, where an earlier version of "Trailing Windmill Sails" first appeared. Thanks also to the Kentucky Arts Council for a generous fellowship that allowed for the completion of this project. Gratitude to Robin Lippincott, Walter McCord, Dean Pearson, and Neela Vaswani, who each read early incarnations of the manuscript, and to Robert and Elizabeth, who were willing to take a chance.

"Better and nimbler than the hand is the thought which wrought through it."

—Emerson

A Note on the Author

KIRBY GANN is the author of *The Barbarian Parade* (Hill Street Press, 2004) and co-editor of the award-winning anthology *A Fine Excess: Contemporary Literature at Play* (Sarabande Books, 2001). His short fiction has received a Special Mention in *The Pushcart Prize* anthology, and has appeared in several journals, including *American Writing*, *The Southeast Review*, and *Witness*. In 2003 he was awarded an artist fellowship from the Kentucky Arts Council. Kirby Gann lives in Louisville, Kentucky, with his wife Stephanie; he is managing editor at Sarabande Books, and also teaches in the brief-residency MFA in Writing Program at Spalding University. He welcomes correspondence and invites readers to visit his Web site, www.kirbygann.net.